School Library Journal (January 1, 2010)

Gr 9 Up–Castrovilla's first young adult novel tackles a number of serious issues including depression, sexual assault, eating disorders, mental illness, cutting, and abandonment. Willow, 15, is sent by her unstable mother to spend the summer on her Aunt Agatha's barge in Rockaway, NY. As Willow and Agatha work on what appears to be a hopeless project, converting the barge into a floating concert hall, Willow finds herself both attracted to and repulsed by the hired hand, Craig. At the same time, she is intrigued by her emerging relationship with mysterious and reclusive Axel, who lives on a sailboat docked close to the barge. Frustrated by Axel's lack of romantic interest, Willow finally accepts Craig's advances but finds herself a victim of sexual assault. Axel intervenes before Willow can be seriously hurt and then assists her through the process of the investigation. Unable to face her aunt, Willow goes back to live with Axel and learns that he cuts himself to deal with the pain caused by his own abandonment and abuse. The sexual scenes with Craig and Willow are descriptive and raw, and the mood is always bleak, at times bordering on melodrama. The plot is predictable and somewhat implausible. However, many readers will quickly forgive all of these flaws as they race to the tidy, yet satisfying fairy-tale ending.–Lynn Rashid, Marriotts Ridge High School, Marriottsville, MD Copyright 2010 Reed Business Information.

SAVED
by the
MUSIC

Dedication

"It is required, you do awake your faith."
— William Shakespeare

For my intrepid aunt, Olga Bloom,
and for me — survivors, both.

Selene Castrovilla

SAVED
by the
MUSIC

WestSide Books
Lodi, New Jersey

Published by WestSide Books
60 Industrial Road
Lodi, NJ 07644
973-458-0485
Fax: 973-458-5289

Library of Congress Control Number: 2009930790

International Standard Book Number: 978-1-934813-14-0
School ISBN: 978-1-934813-30-0
Cover illustration by Michael Morgenstern
Cover design by Chinedum Chukwu & David Lemanowicz
Interior design by David Lemanowicz

Printed in the United States of America
10 9 8 7 6 5 4 3 2 1

First Edition

SAVED

by the

MUSIC

Stranded

The taxi's spinning wheels spit pebbles and dirt as it left me behind at the marina's gate. The dusty haze was a perfect fit for my state of mind.

I wobbled across the driveway and into the marina, trying to balance with my heavy suitcase. Sweat beaded under my bangs.

It was unbearably bright, like the sun was aiming right at me. But looking around, I decided that the marina needed all the brightening it could get. Damaged boats lined the gravel-filled boatyard, all of them in dry dock, up on stilts like big crutches—a nautical hospital. Their exposed insides were like my wrecked life. But at least someone cared enough to fix *them*.

The sounds of saws, drills, and hammers punctured the air as I passed the workers using them. I tried tuning out the men's jeering whistles.

One yelled out, "Nice ass."

Another called, "Hey, Slim."

Some people really get off on taunting strangers.

I crunched through gravel, kicking up pieces as I moved toward the water. Sailboats, cruisers, and yachts were all tied with rope to the docks.

So where was my Aunt Agatha's barge? What did a barge even look like?

Aunt Agatha had told me about the barges that kings rode on centuries before, but she'd never actually described their appearance. There didn't seem to be anything worthy of royalty bobbing about in this marina, at least not anything I saw.

"Over here, Willow!" a scratchy voice called out.

There was Aunt Agatha, waving from the deck of a huge and hideous metal monstrosity. *This blows*, I thought, doubting there'd be any cable TV on this scow.

My aunt hurried off the vile green vessel, prancing along a wooden plank across the water to reach me.

"What is that ugly thing?" I asked.

"This barge is our future concert hall!"

She couldn't be serious.

"It looks like it belongs in the army."

"Darling, a little paint will fix that."

I couldn't believe my bad karma. Instead of staying in the run-down house where I lived with my mother—that is, whenever my mom actually came home—I'd be spending the summer on a steel nightmare. At least, in the house, I had my own room with all my stuff, instead of whatever I could squeeze into my suitcase.

Snatching my giant bag, Aunt Agatha galloped back up the narrow gangplank that stretched from the dock to the barge.

"What are you waiting for, dear heart?" she called. "An invitation?"

I studied the gray, decaying wood of the gangplank, which was still shaking from her running on it.

I couldn't get on that. My aunt was nuts!

Beaming at me with her sunbaked, craggy face, Aunt Agatha looked like a happy walnut. What could she possibly be smiling about? She wore a baggy, paint-splotched sweatshirt and frayed jeans.

Why couldn't she just be normal?

"Hurry up," she urged. "Time's ticking by!"

I eyed the plank again. "You want me to cross the water on that thing? No way!"

"It's the only way, love."

I didn't want to tell Aunt Agatha I was scared.

"Put your mind in the soles of your feet," she said, dancing on the plank.

What did that mean?

Her voice was bursting with enthusiasm, which annoyed the hell out of me. "Don't look down."

So of course I looked down. Yuk! *Could any fish survive in that murk?* A piece of a tire and a crushed milk carton floated by. I shivered. I was next—I just knew it.

"Concentrate, darling. You can do it!"

My gaze returned to the scrawny piece of lumber. *What if it snapped?* I couldn't swim.

I bit my lip and shuffled mentally through my options: (1) Run. (2) Call the authorities. (3) Keep quiet and walk the plank.

If I ran away from the barge, it would be smack into the hellish slum I'd just ridden through, which waited outside the tall barbed wire fence of the boatyard.

I didn't see any pay phones around the god-forsaken marina, and I was about the only one in tenth grade without a cell phone. And that meant I'd have to get on the barge, plank or not. I'd have to go along with Aunt Agatha's demands, at least for now.

She held out her hand as far as she could reach. "Come on, love," she coaxed.

I tried to put my mind in my soles, like she said. I placed one foot on the wood. It quivered. I tried not to quiver, too.

I knelt and began crawling across the creaking, sagging plank. It smelled moldy and felt rough. I held my breath. The plank bounced. My eyes focused on my aunt's insanely happy face, and I forced my body to go on.

"Okay, love!"

Aunt Agatha's outstretched hand waited, just inches away. I lurched forward. The plank shook again as our hands locked. I'd made it.

"Welcome home, darling," she bubbled, giving me a hug.

Home? This place would never be home.

"And remember, things are only obstacles if you perceive them as such," Aunt Agatha added.

Everything was an obstacle. Especially her and her sorry barge.

The Horror Continues

Maybe the inside looked better.

Then Aunt Agatha yanked open the thick metal door of the cabin.

Any hopes I had about the interior being in better shape were swept away in an explosion of dirt and dust. Particles went up my nose and down my throat, sending me into a coughing and sneezing fit.

"Sorry, love. I'll have to remember to clean up around this door," Aunt Agatha said.

Once the cloud cleared, I saw a cavernous chamber—big, dark, and spooky. That's all it was—one huge, bleak steel room, about the size of my school gym, with a regular-size door at either end, and gigantic sliding doors on each side. The walls, floor, and ceiling were covered with grime. And piles of wood cluttered the room, along with all kinds of other construction-type junk.

"What do you think?" Aunt Agatha chirped, propping the door open with a crowbar. "Isn't she a beaut?"

I cleared my throat. "It's not what I pictured."

She laughed. "What is?" She tweaked my nose. "You didn't think the place came all finished, did you?"

She led me to one of the humongous sliding doors. It ran the length of the wall between the ceiling and the floor and took up a good part of the side wall.

"I need your strength to open it," she said.

If she was counting on me for strength, she was in big trouble. But I followed her lead, leaning into the door.

The high-pitched squeal vibrated through me. Slowly, we pushed the door open. By the time we were done, my arms throbbed worse than if I'd done a hundred push-ups. The screeching sound rang in my head.

At least there was light now, but I was near tears. I dropped to the floor. The cold steel sent a chill through my bare legs.

Aunt Agatha closed the front door she'd propped open with a crowbar. Then she flopped down beside me.

"The world thinks I'm completely mad, you know," she said.

You don't say. I can't imagine why. I didn't say these things, but it was like she'd heard them anyway.

"Darling, don't you believe in my vision?"

No, I did not. But she looked so love-struck, I couldn't tell her.

"I do, in theory," I said.

Aunt Agatha frowned. She didn't like halfway, cop-out answers, and she wouldn't let me off that easy. "What do you mean?"

"Well, I think a boat is a cool idea for a concert hall. But . . . I'm not sure that this is the right boat."

"Why not? Chamber music was meant to be played in chambers. Behold: a chamber!"

More like a chamber of horrors.

"Yes, but . . . "

"Royalty listened to classical music on barges floating down the River Thames."

Okay, no way did kings park their butts on any scroungy old boats like this one.

"But look at this place!" I said.

"It just needs some work."

"*Some* work? Oh my God, where do we even begin?" It all seemed so hopeless. I felt the tears coming.

Aunt Agatha took my hand. "Willow, all I'm asking is for you to believe."

Sorry. I was fresh out of hopes and dreams.

I couldn't even look at her. I stared at the water through the open door, watching a straw, still stuck in a plastic lid, and a decaying piece of what looked like lunch meat float by. Fat drops fell from my eyes onto the steel between my legs.

"Dear heart," she said, gripping my hand, "when you look at this barge, you see ugliness. But I see victory. It's taken me years to get here."

Great. Years to get a garbage dump.

A seagull swooped down, let out a screeching "Caw!" and scarfed up the lunch meat.

Aunt Agatha said, "I embarked on this journey when you were born. You actually were the catalyst." She pressed hard, her pulse beating into mine. Still staring at the floating garbage, I tried to blink back the tears.

She went on: "I began my search for a place where beauty could flourish, where music could flow uninterrupted, uncorrupted by the politics and corporations of this world. My only agenda was beauty, finding beauty in the unexpected, bringing it to the masses—and especially to you. For a decade and a half, I've searched for a place to do that, and now, at last, I have one."

Hurray for her.

I didn't turn around.

She said, "It's been an uphill battle, Willow. And I need you to help complete my journey."

God, she was dramatic. She belonged back in ancient Greece with Sophocles or someone. I finally turned my head, but didn't say anything. She let go of my hand and slapped my leg.

"Let's get you settled in. We'll talk more about this later."

Oh, goodie. More fun to look forward to.

Aunt Agatha showed me my so-called bed: a ratty black vinyl-looking couch three-quarters into the room. I sat down, and a spring sprang into my butt. *Fantastic.*

My "bed" was surrounded by mountains of lumber. There were also endless amounts of tools, nails, and other supplies lying around. Stumbling to the bathroom in the middle of the night would be a delight. Speaking of which . . .

"Where's the bathroom?"

"Behind the galley—that's nautical language for kitchen—in the far right corner, up two stairs. But there's one thing. . . . "

Just one?

"The toilet is a gas-operated incinerator. That means it burns up the waste matter. In other words, leave quickly, or hold your nose. And don't use the toilet immediately after someone else. If the embers are still lit and they get wet, your derriere will get a steam bath."

How did the woman come up with this stuff?

"What would you like for dinner?" she asked.

"I brought my own."

"Oh, well, I'll open a can of tuna and join you. Incidentally, there's bottled water and all sorts of canned goods in the galley."

"If you don't mind, I'd like to be alone."

"Fine, fine. Let's close the door, and you can have all the privacy you want. My cot's on the other side of the room."

Once again, I had to huff and heave, this time closing the door. I wished we hadn't bothered to open it in the first place. That was just like Aunt Agatha. She looked for hard work. It seemed like her mission was to make everything as difficult as possible.

"Does anyone else work here?" I asked.

"I've got a boy from the yard helping me out," she said as the door closed on the last sliver of daylight, leaving us in complete darkness. *How special.*

"Hold on, hold on, love. I always forget to turn on the light beforehand." She climbed over all the junk on the floor

15

without tripping once and popped on the light—a dark brown, sad-looking ceramic garage-sale number with a beat-up, bent tan shade.

I stumbled over the debris, sank onto the couch, and buried my face in my stinging hands. A weak ring of yellow light from the sickly lamp circled me and the couch, putting me center stage in a room full of gloom.

A boy from the yard, a woman who was no spring chicken, and I were going to turn a steel atrocity into a place people would actually want—even pay—to go.

Right. Not unless a magic wand was involved.

If only I could click my sneaker heels three times and go home.

Scraps

There was nothing to do but sleep.

Except I couldn't even do that.

It was beyond creepy on that saggy couch, surrounded by plywood and power tools and noises. A scraping. A swoosh. A bang. Now I wished Aunt Agatha wasn't at the other end of the barge, separated from me by all that junk.

I shifted and turned, trying to find a comfortable position. The motion of the barge was making me a little nauseous. I hadn't noticed it before, and it wasn't like the barge was rocking. Instead, the feeling was more of a fluttering, so slight that it almost wasn't there.

I pounded on the sides of the couch cushion—the closest thing I had to a pillow—to fluff it. But it was still a lump. I pulled the flimsy brown checkered blanket higher, up to my neck, wishing that I could just yank it over my head and disappear.

The sounds got louder. What was causing them? Were the piles of things shifting from the tide? Were water rats scurrying around? Eeew.

The darkness freaked me out, too. I couldn't see past

the ring of light the lamp made around me and my "bed." The inky hollow emptiness reminded me of my own. Sometimes I felt as meaningful as a scrap of paper.

Of course, sometimes scrap paper has value. It could be the raw material a playwright uses to scrawl his latest vision. It could be the tool some girl uses to jot down her phone number for the gorgeous guy she just met. It could be the start of something big. But it will probably get tossed in the garbage. And the playwright will probably get lousy reviews. And the gorgeous guy probably will never call.

It's all how you look at things.

I looked at things in the worst way possible. That way, there wouldn't be any disappointment.

This could all be traced back to my name.

How could anyone called Willow be substantial? I swayed, I bent, I folded with the weight of the rain bearing down on me. *What kind of a whooshy, wishy-washy, spill-your-guts-and-weep kind of name is Willow, anyway?*

I bet my mom did that to me on purpose. She wanted to saddle me with a wimp name so she could bask in the sunlight. Isadora, that's her name. Why would an Isadora make a Willow? To stomp all over her, that's why.

Once, I was sitting on my bed, surrounded by my many admirers—rock stars plastered all over my walls to cover the awfully bright, blind-your-eyes yellow paint that was covering the awfully bright, makes-you-want-to-puke green paint that was on the walls before that. I was rocking a bit, singing, "That's me in the corner."

"Did you write a song, Willow?" Mom moved into the room like an unpredicted storm front.

"No, Mom. It's an old R.E.M. song," I answered.

"Oh, it sounded like something you'd say," she commented. Then she was gone. It's like she encourages depression.

My mother spent a lot of my childhood exposing me to life's possibilities: the opera, the stage, classes in art, journalism . . . you name it. But it all just made me feel crappier. That's because I knew, deep inside, that I'd never be able to do any of those things. It wasn't possible. I was like a stray dog with her face pushed against a restaurant window, begging for scraps. *See, scraps again.*

I was really good at hiding how I felt. At school, I faked everyone out by being an overachiever of sorts. They thought I was excelling, but I was actually accelerating. You can't get ambushed if you keep moving. So I studied like a fiend and belonged to six clubs. This way, I got to fit in with everybody—sort of. But I was more of an observer than a participant, to be totally honest.

What I did was zero in on one person in each group, whether I was in a classroom, club, or whatever. Someone who was needy, someone who was shifting his or her eyes around, searching for salvation. You know the type, a person just short of bifocals and pocket protector. We'd bond out of necessity. Except they didn't know that I was needy. I didn't give anything away, and they were just relieved that I wanted to talk to them.

As for everyone else, they saw me, yet they didn't see me. On the school newspaper, they'd ask me to help edit something. In French club, they'd ask me for the correct pronunciation that they couldn't quite get. In poetry club, they'd ask me if their verses flowed the way they should. Everyone came to me for advice and help, but that was it. There was no real connection.

Everyone thought I was going to be something big and important, but I knew I'd probably wind up alone in the forest talking to chipmunks. It was ironic. Because it was such a damn effort to play the game, to put on a front all the time. I wanted to let loose the real me—insecurities, phobias, and all—and let them all know the truth.

And let's face it, the only thing that was going to be big was my fat lump of a body, which no guy in his right mind would ever want to touch. My stupid diet wasn't working. . . .

Enough! I had to get these toxic thoughts out of my brain—before I threw myself overboard. So I did the only thing I could do to drown out the dark: I slid on my headphones and hit play on my iPod. Closing my eyes, I let my version of a lullaby, the deep tones of Jim Morrison—my favorite singer—do their job.

I hate my mother.

I woke up in the dark with a stiff neck and that thought in my head: *I hate my mother. She ditched me.*

I stumbled over the crap on the floor and turned on the lamp. Was it day or night? Who could tell? The steel room looked exactly the same. My cell.

I lay back down, trying again to bunch up the cushion and make it bearable. *Hopeless, just like everything else.*

Why couldn't I stay home this summer? I'd been alone since second grade, 'til eight or nine o'clock every night. On weekends, I'd put myself to bed. I didn't complain. I didn't cry. So why couldn't I be home now? I would've stayed out of her way. All I had in this world was my room, and now I didn't even have that.

All because of Steve.

"Morning, love," Aunt Agatha sang from behind me, shaking me out of my thoughts. "Did you sleep well?"

"Sure," I lied. I turned toward the back of the couch and swiped at my eyes. Then I faced her.

"You slept through my practicing. That's tough to do."

"I was tired."

"Let's get some coffee and get to work."

"I don't drink coffee, Aunt Agatha."

"You don't?"

"No. I'm fifteen."

She looked puzzled. "I drank coffee at ten, darling. You don't know what you're missing. But fine, you can have hot chocolate and a buttered roll from the coffee truck."

"No, thanks. Do they have carrots?"

"Carrots?"

"I mostly eat carrots for breakfast. I'm on a diet."

She looked me up and down. "Darling, you don't need a diet anymore. You've lost too much weight. You look like a rail."

Who was she kidding? I looked more like a railroad. "I'm on a diet, and I eat carrots for breakfast," I said.

"All right. After I have my coffee, I'll head to the supermarket. Make me a list of what you'd like." She sat next to me. "Listen, kiddo. Maybe you don't want to be here, but here you are. I'm not such a bad guy, you know." She rapped me on the shoulder.

I nodded, swallowing the lump in my throat.

She left, and I put my music on again. I never thought I'd want to be home, but I would've given anything to be back on my bed, staring at my huge poster of Jim Morrison. His shaggy, reddish brown hair was just short of long. His face had substance. It was strong, powerful, daring. His muscular arms were outstretched, reaching for me, offering something I just couldn't grab. And his eyes. . . . In his eyes, I saw poetry. The poster said "An American Poet." And that's what he was.

I'd found the poster two years before in my cousin Doug's basement, in a pile of stuff of past lives. His mom was trashing it. "Who's Jim Morrison?" I asked, impressed by the hunk I'd unrolled.

"The lead singer for the Doors," he answered.

"Who are the Doors?"

He stared for a moment, then said, "Oh, yeah, I forgot. Your mom's into opera and junk like that." He gave me a sympathetic look through his oval-rimmed glasses. "They were a band from the sixties. Mom was big into them. Come upstairs, and I'll play you one of their albums.

He played me a song called "Break on Through."

I was captivated.

Not by the music, which included a redundant organy sound. (I soon discovered that the organ was their trademark instrument.)

Not by his voice, which, though powerful, could have stood some training.

It was his words. They hypnotized me. They were the truth. In fact, "Break on Through" eerily described that "inside looking outside" feeling I carried with me.

We listened to Jim Morrison and the Doors all afternoon. Doug told me all about Jim, how he was this brilliant, tortured soul. Jim died mysteriously in France when he was only twenty-seven. Some people thought he'd faked his death. This was all very exciting.

On my way out, I clomped down the basement stairs and saved Jim from a trip to the garbage dump.

The beginning of a beautiful relationship.

I checked out the back-door exit from the room. It led to a rear deck, which looked the same as the front deck: brown rust.

I stared at the other boats. They seemed so content, bobbing along out there. There were yachts, sailboats, cabin cruisers. . . . Why'd I end up standing on a filthy, ugly, godforsaken barge?

Closing my eyes, I choked back the scream inside me. When I opened them again, I saw him.

People Are Strange

He stood on the outer ledge of a sailboat called *Perchance to Dream*. Long straggly hair fell across his slumped shoulders. Standing outside the boat's rail, staring into the water like he was about to jump, he was a dead ringer for the dead Jim Morrison.

A teenage Jim.

He had that same deep-eyed, hollow look that stared back at me from every Doors album cover. A lost look.

Wow, something heavy was sure on his mind.

He noticed me. Studied me. I freaked.

I ran back inside the barge, stubbing my toe against a big black metal thing in the way. Sucking in my pain, I shoved the thick door closed and leaned against it, my heart in overdrive.

Aunt Agatha dropped a ten-pound bag of carrots on the crate that was her coffee table. "That ought to hold you,"

she said, handing me a peeler. "I'll get the rest of the supplies later."

I wondered how she'd manage to get everything across the plank, but not enough to ask.

"Are you ready to work?"

I shrugged.

"Love, I could let you sit here and sulk, but I want to teach you how to enjoy life."

"Enjoy life?" I scoffed. "Fat chance, in here."

"When you create beauty, that's enjoying life." Aunt Agatha beamed.

"Whatever," I said.

"Besides, the time will go faster if you occupy your mind." She winked and headed to her "work table," two sawhorses with a piece of plywood balanced across them. Lying on top was a long, skinny piece of wood. It was a nauseating green, not unlike the original color of my room. "What do you think of this?" she asked.

She didn't want to know. "What's to think about? It's an ugly piece of wood."

"Is it, love?" She grabbed a thick paintbrush, dunked it in a can, and spread clear, thick glop over the green. Then she traded the brush for a flat-bladed tool. She scraped away the paint, sliding it down the long strip until it was a sticky clump on the floor.

"Behold . . . beauty!"

I had to admit, the wood was a beautiful mix of brown and cream. But so what?

"Paint remover, dear heart. It's that simple."

Too bad I couldn't remove Steve from my house with that stuff.

"Imagine, all this mahogany entombed under someone's idea of decor. It came from the old Staten Island Ferry. They were going to throw it all away!" She grabbed up another piece and glopped it up. "And now, we're excavating it."

Good lord. Who did she think she was, that Howard Carter guy who dug up King Tut?

"Here's the plan," she continued. "You're going to strip the wood. I'm going to stain it. And Craig is going to . . . "

The metal door squealed open, interrupting her. "Yooooooo . . ." echoed through the chamber.

"Ah, Craig. I was just telling my niece Willow about you," Aunt Agatha said to a tall guy in a torn red T-shirt covered in paint splatters and frayed cutoff jeans in the same condition. His long black hair was pulled back in a ponytail, and he wore black sunglasses—like he had to be cool at all costs.

Those shades looked asinine in the dimness of the room we stood in. *Schmuck.*

I had to admit, though, he was hot. His biceps, triceps, quads, or whatever the names of arm and chest muscles are, all screamed "squeeze me." He was raw, rough, ready.

Why did all the hot guys have to be such punks?

"Yo," he said.

Nice command of the English language.

He nodded at Aunt Agatha, then turned to me, lowering his sunglasses to give me the once-over with his big

26

brown eyes. Real smooth. "Yo," he said to me, eyebrows raised.

Terrific.

This was the kind of guy who paid attention to me. I was not a person to him. I was a potential lay.

Other guys talked to me, sure. I actually got along better with them than girls. But I was just their friend. No, I was their advice columnist. "Dear Willow." They all came to me with their problems with girls and everything else.

"Willow, this is Craig Culligan." Aunt Agatha introduced us. "Craig, Willow Moon."

"Charmed," I said.

"Yo," he said.

Did he know any other words?

"He's the boy from the yard I told you about. Starting tomorrow, he's going to be hanging mahogany strips on the walls."

"Across the whole room?" I followed the long length of steel panels, horrified by the amount of days it would take. Days of me and Craig stuck together.

"And across the floor. Pieced together, like a giant mahogany jigsaw puzzle." Aunt Agatha beamed at the thought.

Craig leered at me. It was going to be a long, long summer.

Aunt Agatha headed to her workstation on the other end of the barge. She had a pile of "excavated" wood waiting.

I could tell she thought she was doing me a favor, leaving me alone with this guy. Like I needed companionship or something. *As if.*

I put on my headphones and started chipping and stripping away. Of course, Mr. Wonderful suddenly wanted to talk. Apparently, he had nothing to do but hang around. *Imagine that.*

I tried to ignore him, but he got in my face.

So close I could smell the testosterone wafting from his pores.

Mental face slap! *Hold out for a guy who doesn't throw the girl out with the condom*, I told myself.

He said something. I pointed to the headphones. "I CAN'T HEAR YOU," I shouted.

He yanked them off. I didn't know what to say.

"So, where you from?"

I'm from a place where we form complete sentences. "Long Island," I answered, as clipped as possible. I stared at the strip, avoiding eye contact.

"Whadaya think a Rockaway?"

"Well, I haven't had the pleasure of exploring the neighborhood yet," I said, putting my finished strip aside and starting another, longer one. "But I was impressed by the burned-out, boarded-up buildings I passed along the way."

He didn't say anything. Probably took a few minutes to process that many words.

"Yo," he said finally. "Ya gotta be careful 'round the 'hood."

Yeah, I kind of got that.

"I'll take ya out for pizza, show ya 'round," he continued.

"I don't eat pizza." I shoved at the gunk hard, pushing it down, down, down.

"Huh?" I guessed in his world, pizza was a dietary staple, like rice in China.

"How 'bout Mickey Dee's?"

How about no?

"Look, Craig," I said. "I'm not allowed to go wandering around unfamiliar neighborhoods."

"Why not?"

I slammed the scraper against the wood in exasperation. "I'm fifteen."

"So? My sister's twelve. She goes wherever the hell she wants."

Super.

Actually, I could go wherever I wanted at home. I was about as supervised as an alley cat. There were no rules. But all the other kids had them.

"Well, back in the Five Towns, parents like to check out where their kids are hanging out. Crazy, huh?"

Another strip done. I pushed at my sleeves and gunked up another one.

He looked confused. "I'll protect you." *But who would protect me from him?*

I tried something else. "You look a little old for me."

"I'm twenty."

"Did you not hear me when I said I was fifteen?" I dropped a huge pile of green gook onto the floor.

"Yeah, so?"

29

"Hmmm . . . fifteen, twenty. Anything wrong with that?"

"We're not gettin' married, just havin' some fun."

That's what I was afraid of.

"Oy vey," I sighed.

"Huh?"

I forgot I wasn't looking at him, so I looked up. "That's what the Jews say, instead of 'Jesus Christ.'" God, those glasses were annoying. Like speaking to someone in a motorcycle visor.

He moved in closer, examining me like I was an alien. *Testosterone alert.* "You Jewish?"

"No."

He scratched his head. "Then why you talkin' Jewish?"

I shrugged. "Almost everyone else in the Five Towns is Jewish. You just pick it up. Like you picked up your stunning vocabulary."

He blinked at me. Again, I'd loaded too many words on him at once.

"So what are ya?"

What was I? Good question.

"What I am is tired. And I have a headache. So, see ya!" I gave him a curt wave with my spatula.

"We'll head out tomorrow after work," he said with a wink. Was he a brick or what?

I just turned and walked away.

I sat on the front deck and stared at the garbage floating at the edge of the deck. More scraps.

Talking about religion sent me right back behind my elementary school gates—those tall metal bars that are supposed to keep kids safe. In no time, I was there.

❋

Standing in the playground, shuffling my Keds in the dirt, in this new place. A new beginning.

It's the first day of second grade. We'd just moved from Woodside, Queens. From a project where incinerator smoke always clawed my throat. Where the drug dealers were waiting on the playground.

It's exciting, being in this new place, the Five Towns. Aunt Agatha lent Mom money for the house in Atlantic Beach. The town's tiny, smaller than the massive maze of dirty brick apartment buildings we came from.

Atlantic Beach is so small, there's no school there. We have to ride the bus to Lawrence, across the bay.

There are no drug dealers by the fence at recess.

But there is a group of kids waiting for me. Different heights, looks like a few could be in fourth or fifth grade.

"So, what are you?" a really tall boy asks.

"What?"

"Jewish or Catholic?"

He could be speaking French for all I understand. I don't know what to say.

"Well?" a medium-sized girl in ponytails asks.

I still don't know what to say. "What's Jewish and Catholic?"

They all stare at me. The tall boy says, "You don't know your religion? What are you, a moron?"

Okay, I don't know what that word means, either—religion, not moron. I want to cry, but I don't.

"You celebrate Christmas or Hanukkah?"

"Christmas." What was Hanukkah? Didn't everyone get presents under their Christmas tree?

"Catholic," yells a short girl.

"Really?" I ask, relieved.

The tall boy isn't convinced. He continues, "You go to church?"

"No."

"Temple?"

"No."

They start shooting questions at me from all sides. About Jesus and God—words I know only from grown-ups yelling.

Jewish or Catholic, I have to be one or the other.

I'm nothing.

I ride the bus home, watch TV, and try to forget about my first day at the new school I'd been so excited about.

When Mom comes home, when she finally comes home way after dark, I ask her what I am.

"Tell them you're agnostic," she says.

But that wasn't one of the choices.

When I go back the next day, I tell everyone I'm half Jewish, half Catholic.

Nice try, but a little late. That was my first attempt to

32

fit in with everyone. I could have used some advance warning to figure all this out. Turned out most of the kids were Jewish, so that would have been the better choice. But who knew?

The Catholics were a tight, tough little bunch.

I wound up fitting in with no one. I ate lunch alone that year, at the last table in the cafeteria. In the corner. The beginning of the story of my life.

Back on the playground in second grade, I learned I couldn't fit in religion-wise, the same day I learned what religion even was.

Now I had another plan.
I needed to ditch my virginity.

That night I lay on the couch, thinking. I was sick of being a virgin. Forget about virginity, I'd never even kissed a guy.

I just knew things would be better if I wasn't a virgin. I wouldn't feel so apart. I saw the girls who "did it." They were popular, always laughing, always part of the big crowd. Never alone.

Never.

I reviewed my options for de-virginization. There weren't many.

Actually, there was one. One leering, crude imbecile.

But Craig was hot, so why not? It wasn't like we were going to get married, like I'd be stuck with him. What was the problem?

The problem was, I couldn't stand guys like Craig. They were users. But they were also the only guys who paid attention to me.

The problem was, I kind of wanted someone to want me for me, not just for what they could get from me.

Maybe that was too much to ask.

Maybe, I thought, I should go have some fun with Craig.

I woke up with a jolt, jumping from the couch. It was still nighttime. At least, I thought it was. Who could tell in that pit?

But Aunt Agatha wasn't bustling around yet, so it was probably still dark. For as long as I could remember, she'd risen with the sun and practiced her fiddle. That was her thing.

I'd fallen asleep in the work clothes Aunt Agatha had given me—a baggy blue man's dress shirt and some kind of beat-up white pants that were also huge. The faint smell of paint remover coming from them was making me sick. I needed some air.

Once past my ring of light, I had to inch my way to the back door to avoid getting killed on some lurking hazard. I tried pulling the handle up slowly so as not to disturb Aunt Agatha, but it made a banging sound anyway. She didn't wake up, though. I pushed through the door, slow, slow, try-ing not to let it creak. It did, but only a little.

I breathed in the cool night air and stared at the sky. The moon hung so low, it was like being close to the heav-ens. Like I could take a leap and be there.

The last thing you'd expect in Far Rockaway, Queens.

I identified with the moon. For one thing, it was my last name. But it was more than that. The moon looked translucent, and sometimes I felt like that, too. Not trans-parent, but not solid either—kind of halfway there. The dark water sloshed against the barge, rocking it gently. Ahead of me, the moon illuminated patches of ocean in spots, which looked like they were dancing.

For the first time, I relaxed. Just a little.

I turned to get my iPod so I could chill outside for a while, but suddenly there was this low, kind of haunting music coming from somewhere. It was deeper than a vio-lin. Someone was playing a cello. A classical piece—don't ask me what, because I couldn't have told the difference between Bach and Beethoven if someone had held a gun to my head—whatever it was, it was nice. Soothing. It rolled over the waves, like the ocean was singing a love song. A sad love song.

Go figure. Two musicians in one hellhole.

I flicked my eyes across the dozens of boats floating on the waves. They stopped at the sailboat *Perchance to Dream.*

Make that two musicians—and a boy who looked like Jim Morrison.

Crybaby

The next morning, Aunt Agatha's practicing did wake me up. I'd been dreaming about cello music, and then a violin broke in.

I slid off the couch and went to watch her. When I was little, she used to visit every week to give me a lesson. I hated it! She had to bribe me with loose change for every line I played. She finally gave up because I never practiced. Mom never pushed me on it; she was too busy in her own little world.

The violin was Aunt Agatha's thing, but it wasn't mine. It took her about five years to see that. And by then, she was paying me in dollars.

Today, my aunt was deep in concentration, focused on the sheet music open on her stand. Her bow perched near the bridge of her fiddle, and back and forth it went, never hesitating, never losing its balance. She was playing something I recognized.

I clapped when she finished.

She turned, surprised. "I didn't see you there, Willow."

"I remember that piece. Who wrote it?"

"Chopin. You always enjoyed Chopin."

"Oh, yeah, that's right." I don't know why, but I felt embarrassed all of a sudden. I looked down at my feet.

"Dear heart, I want to talk with you."

Her soft voice made me feel like bursting into tears.

"I didn't know your mother wasn't going to drive you here the other day. I would've picked you up."

I studied an interesting diamond pattern in the steel floor.

"Willow, your mother loves you, you know. She just has problems."

The tears were making circles over the diamonds.

"Willow, will you look at me?"

I shook my head no.

Her folding chair scraped against the floor. Then she wrapped my hand in hers, rough, wrinkly skin against mine.

"It's not your fault, Willow."

She squeezed tighter, tighter. "Your father couldn't help her. He tried. . . . "

I twisted my hand from her grasp and looked up. "I don't want to hear about *him*."

Licking at the tears that were dripping into my mouth, I hurried into the bathroom.

I came out when I felt the barge moving. Craig had arrived and was hacking at some wood—a sleazeball with a saw. He gave me a wave with it.

The barge lurched. "What's going on?" I asked, un-
nerved.

Aunt Agatha looked up from the wood she was brushing stain onto. "A towboat's moving us to a closer berth. I
realized that if I didn't pay for a spot right on the dock, you
wouldn't see land all summer."

"No more plank?"

She smiled. "No more plank."

"Gee, thanks." I gave her a little smile back.

"You're welcome, dear heart. Now go have breakfast.
Did you have dinner last night?" She raised her eyebrows
at me.

"Yeah."

"Really? How many meals did you pack in that bag of
yours?"

"I have these bars that you eat instead of regular food.
They're fine. They're good."

Craig was watching me from behind her. He didn't
have his shades on. Guess it wouldn't be too cool to slice
off a finger he couldn't see.

Aunt Agatha frowned. "I don't think you're getting the
proper nutrition. But we'll talk about that later." She turned
back to her project.

"Listen, when we get to the new spot, would it be okay
if I went for a walk?"

She swung her head to answer. "Of course. You're not
a captive here, and you don't have to do anything you don't
want to. Remember that."

"I could show ya around," said Craig. "If ya wait 'til later," he added, seeing the look on Aunt Agatha's face. She didn't like slacking, bless her.

"I'd like to go by myself," I said. That was true, and it was also a lie.

Later, I sat on the couch and crunched on a carrot, trying to think about getting off the barge. But my mind went back to my dad. Why did Aunt Agatha have to bring up her no-good brother?

My father ran out on us when I was six. When he left, he told me he was sorry, but he just couldn't take my mother anymore.

But he didn't take me with him, either.

My mom's reaction was to set off into a slew of insults, then and whenever Dad's name came up: "Your father's useless." "A bastard." "A piece of crap."

I laid on my bed, pressing into my cushion and soaking it with tears, the lesson that my dad hadn't wanted me sinking in deeper each time I thought about it. My dad was gone for good, and I was alone with Mom, who had a different personality for every day of the week.

And still does today, I thought as I clutched Aunt Agatha's lumpy couch cushion against my stomach. A voice inside me said, *You're such a baby, Willow. Quit wallowing and go to sleep.*

So I did.

After spending two days floating on the barge, it felt kind of weird to be walking on land again. There wasn't much to see in the boatyard—just more of what I'd seen already. But it beat being on the barge with Mr. Conversation.

It sure was hot, though. I had my hair pulled back in a ponytail, but I wished I had a stretchy thing to get my bangs off my face. All around the marina, red-faced men of varying ages endured the sun's punishment as they hammered, sawed, or sanded away. Again, I was bombarded with whistles and insults as I walked.

"Hey, sexy."

"A little more meat on that ass, and you could be a supermodel."

Why was hurting someone such a popular sport?

I didn't react or run. Instead, I put on my iPod headphones and listened to Jim sing "My Eyes Have Seen You" and thought of that boy on the boat.

I tramped around the boatyard, breathing in the salty air and checking out the boats on stilts. My white sneakers were soon speckled brown with dirt.

The shoreline overlooked the boats in the water, and I went to sit on a wooden bench facing the docks. Again, my eyes wandered over to that sailboat, *Perchance to Dream*.

I wondered if that boy on the boat was okay now. He'd looked so sad when I saw him the first time.

"Ahem." Behind me, someone cleared their throat. "Excuse me, miss . . ."

I turned around and faced a shrimpy guy wearing a red "Manny's Groceries" cap and carting two bags of groceries, one in each hand. Looking like they might outweigh him, the bags seemed like they were slipping from his grasp. The guy himself was wobbling a little, as if he couldn't balance his body between the bags.

"Yes?" I asked him.

"Do you know where the . . ." He stopped, maneuvering the bag in his left hand so that he could read the paper he clutched. "Do you know where the Ridge boat is?"

I shook my head no.

He squinted at the paper again. "Axel . . . Axel Ridge?"

"No, sorry."

He sighed heavily and looked at the paper for a third time. "*Perchance to Dream*?" How about that? That's the name of the boat this guy lives on."

"Oh, yes. It's over there," I said. I pointed to the boat, and the delivery guy hobbled off, staggering under his load but somehow managing to keep the bags in his scrawny arms.

So now I knew the name of either the boy or his dad. *Axel . . . interesting name.*

"Yo." I felt a sudden burst of hot breath on my neck.

Terrific. I spun around. "Hello, Craig."

"There's that rich dude," he said, nodding toward the boat where the delivery guy was handing off the groceries to the boy—Axel.

"You know him?" I asked.

"Naw, not personal or nothin'. Everyone talks about him 'round here, sayin' that he's loaded."

"He lives on that boat with his parents?"

"Naw," he said again. "He lives alone."

"Alone? But he looks like a teenager."

Craig shrugged. "His dad is this mega rich dude that owns a ton of them buildings in New York."

I remembered the last name and took a guess: "Wade Ridge?"

"That's the dude," Craig agreed.

"But I don't understand. Why would Wade Ridge's son live *here*? He could afford to live anywhere he wants."

"It's wacked," Craig agreed. "But the guy's wacked, too. He never even gets off his boat."

"Never?"

"I never seen him off of it. He gets food delivered to him; his clothes're picked up and cleaned. Nice ta have bucks, huh?"

"I guess."

Meanwhile, Craig had edged himself closer and closer, to the point where we were practically touching.

I took a step back. "Well, I'm going for a walk."

"I gotta get some shit at the hardware store for Aggie." He gave me a wink. "Catcha later."

Not if I run fast enough.

Still thinking about the mysterious Axel, I rounded a corner past a big cabin cruiser, suspended in what looked like a huge sling, with the name *Maritime Bliss* painted in blue block letters on its rear. I couldn't get Axel's eyes out of my mind. Even from the distance between us when I'd first spotted him, I could almost see myself in those eyes.

That made me damn nervous.

But what did I have to worry about? I never went looking for people, that's for sure.

So if Axel Ridge never got off his boat, I guess I was never gonna meet him. There. That took a whole lot of pressure off.

That's when he stepped into my path.

Stumbling Block

I walked right into him. Bam!—and fell on my butt into pebbly dirt, sending up dust clouds. I sat up, blinking up at him through the haze, trying to look casual. Hard to do, especially because the face in front of me was the face I'd stared at from my bed for the past two years—he was Jim Morrison's double.

And then there was that other thing—what I'd felt when he'd first looked at me from his boat: that feeling of being beckoned. . . .

"Are you all okay?" His voice was low and quick. He didn't look right at me. It was more like somewhere off to the right of me.

I nodded dumbly. With a halfway glance, he offered me his hand, but I got myself up on my own. I was coated with sand. I probably looked like a giant breaded pork chop.

Not that it mattered what I looked like, because he now seemed fascinated with the ground. He kicked into it with his sneaker, creating smaller clouds than my butt had generated.

"I'm Axel," he said, after a few moments of staring at dirt.

"I'm Willow," I said, extending my hand kind of low, so he'd see it.

He took it and shook. A sensation passed through me when we touched, like static shock, yet somehow pleasant. He must have felt it, too, because he actually looked at me. There was still the same sadness in his green eyes that I'd seen before.

He didn't say anything else.

Boy, we were in trouble if he was depending on me to start talking. But I gave it a shot.

"So what are you doing off your boat?" I asked.

He shoved his hands into the pockets of his cutoff jeans and looked back down. I'd said the wrong thing, apparently. *How unusual.*

More moments went by. Axel dug pebbles from the dirt with his feet and shifted from one foot to another.

I read his faded, frayed-sleeved T-shirt and wondered where "Midland Prep" was. *And if they taught language skills there.*

"I was looking for you," he finally said.

"Me?" Just to clarify, as he might have been addressing the stones he was still admiring.

"Yeah. I . . . I wanted to know why . . . why you ran away from me yesterday."

His words were a strange combination of hesitancy and speed. He ran his fingers through his disheveled brown hair.

I wanted to know the same thing myself.

"I just have poor people skills, I guess."

He smiled briefly at that.

"Me, too."

He scanned the sky, taking great interest in a passing plane overhead. This was some conversation. But I was afraid to try again, having tasted my foot once already.

Finally, he looked at me. And there it was again—that feeling of being pulled, like a metal shard to a magnet.

We looked at each other a little longer. He fidgeted a little, kicked his feet some more.

"Well, see you around, I guess," he said.

"I guess."

Head lowered, he walked away, disappearing between the boats.

I headed back to the barge, jostling a question around in my head.

What the hell was wrong with Axel Ridge?

When I climbed the new ladder back onto the barge—boy, I never thought I'd be so grateful for a ladder!—Craig was still mercifully absent. But Aunt Agatha had company.

She was sitting by the open side door, fiddle perched upright on her lap, the bottom pushing into her leg, the top clutched in her hand. She was telling five little boys—they all had to be around seven or eight years old—about the life of the composer Paganini.

"Paganini was probably the most popular and well-paid violinist of all time. People paid $300 a ticket to hear him. They thought he was either magical or possessed by the devil because his music was so marvelous and unlike anything they'd ever heard. He composed it himself, and it was very difficult to play. People have been struggling with it ever since—hence, my practicing today!"

The boys stared at her, wide-eyed. Aunt Agatha knew how to tell a story, for sure.

The boys finally headed out in a row, clanging down the new steel ladder as each bounced behind the other.

"Hey, kiddo," Aunt Agatha said, seeing me. "Looks like we're going to have a lot more visitors now that our gangplank is history."

She looked me up and down and asked with a twinkle, "Take a roll in the mud?"

"Not on purpose," I answered. "Where's the shower, anyway?"

"Shower?" she echoed, like the word was foreign. "Darling, we have no shower. This isn't a resort, you know."

Yeah, I got that. But I didn't consider showers a luxury.

"So how do I get this dirt off?"

"Soap and sponge, dear heart."

She said the words so matter-of-factly. Two days ago, I would've flipped, but now I just accepted it. I guess you could adapt to anything.

"All righty then," I said, heading for the sink.

I sat on the couch, ready to slip on my iPod and listen to some Jim. I must've been awfully tired, because next thing I knew I was waking up in the middle of the night with drool dripping from the side of my mouth.

Again, I felt stifled.

Again, I needed air.

I did my inching and stumbling act again, heading to the back deck of the barge.

Once I was outside, the sounds of the cello summoned me, like a friend in trouble. The music was stormy this time, striking frenzied notes in my head. Clouds dashed across the moonless sky, almost as if they were keeping the frantic tempo.

I spotted a light on in one of the boats.

Suddenly, I had a crazy idea where the music was coming from. And I wasn't going to wait 'til morning to find out if I was right.

Expedition

I skulked along the rocking dock to the boat and tried to see in a window. I wasn't tall enough, so I stood on my toes. Even doing that, I still wasn't tall enough, so I leaned against the boat, gripping its ledge to pull myself higher.

The boat moved.

"Aghhhh!" I screamed, as I was pulled from the dock. I dangled from the ledge, helpless.

I tried to pull myself up. My muscles burned from the effort, but I failed.

Jumping back down looked impossible. If I fell into the water, I could be crushed between the dock and the boat. Besides, I couldn't swim. How long could I hold on?

A set of hands came from above and locked onto my wrists. Warm, strong hands.

They pulled, and I went up. My skin rubbed against the cold, smooth fiberglass, and a chill shot through me to my spine. My arms felt like they were being yanked from their sockets. I slid over the top, my body rolling across the thin metal railing as I flopped onto the deck: Willow, the catch of the day.

My fingers traced the grain of the wooden deck grate-fully. Trembling and gasping, I looked up. "Th- th-thanks."

Axel looked pissed.

"May I ask, what the fuck is wrong with you?"

Good to see he was getting over the timid thing.

"Next time, could you just knock?"

This was a new Axel. One who spoke. One who could be sarcastic. One like—me.

He led me down the hatchway steps and offered me a seat on one of the two couches attached to the walls facing each other, and wrapped a blanket around me. Then he picked up a black T-shirt from the floor and slid it on, but not before I noticed some decent-sized slash marks across his chest and stomach—like he'd gone a few rounds with a box cutter.

After I warmed up, we moved to benches at his table, also attached to the wall. The benches were bolted to the floor.

"So, you always prowl around at one o'clock in the morning?"

"No, I never even leave my room at home, except to go to school. Kind of like you and this boat." I remained a master of obnoxious observations.

Axel's change in behavior might have had something to do with the citrus-flavored vodka he was kicking back shots of. He'd slugged down two in the few minutes we'd sat there. "Want some?"

I shook my head no. "How can you get liquor? You're not twenty-one, are you?"

He laughed. "You kidding? You think they proof

around here? I call up, and they deliver it for an extra ten. They'd sell it to a two-year-old if he had the cash and could make the call."

"Do you realize you said more to me just now than in our whole first conversation?"

He tossed another shot down.

"Getting to know you, now," he replied.

Getting to know the bottom of the bottle was more like it.

"I'm eighteen, incidentally," he said.

Behind him, behind me, and everywhere else were shelves and stacks of books. Only one side of the cabin—the galley—was bookless.

"You want something to drink?" he asked.

"I'll take some tea."

"A tea totaler, huh?"

"Well, I *am* fifteen."

He laughed again.

"What's so funny?" I asked.

"Nothing. You're right, you're right. It's just that all the fifteen-year-olds I've ever known—from Park Avenue to this dump—would never turn down a shot in favor of tea." His words tottered a bit.

"Whatever," I grumbled.

"Don't get pissy. I like that about you." He smiled, lopsided and dimpled.

Pretty heart-stopping.

He puttered around his galley, stumbling a few times, searching for the tea. The area was small, about the size of a closet. It was all done in shiny black granite.

Finally, he managed to put a mug of steaming tea in front of me. He threw the box of tea bags into a drawer.

"Safely stowed," he said with a wobbly chuckle.

Actually, I felt a little wobbly myself. You really knew you were floating on a sailboat. This was no fluttering. We were bobbing. Up, down; up, down.

Axel sat back down across from me and took another shot. He hiccuped, and then his face turned really serious.

"Not to sound parental or anything, but don't ever do anything like that again. You could've been killed."

He did sound parental, but his 80-proof breath overrode his voice. He took my hand in his and squeezed.

Jesus, was this the guy who could barely look at me before?

He sucked in some air, like he was getting ready. I could tell this was going to be an Aunt Agatha–type talk. That's if Aunt Agatha ever decided to belt down a bottle or two.

"This yard is fenced in for a reason. At night, they lock the gate to keep trouble out—get my drift?"

I nodded.

Axel said, "So don't go looking for trouble inside."

Yeesh, that was so an Aunt Agatha line. Delivered slurred and with breath that could halt a charging rhino.

"You're awfully deep for an eighteen-year-old," I said, uncomfortable in his ultra-tight grip. *Off the deep end was what I meant.*

What was really bugging me, though, was this bubbling chemical sensation inside—a powerful reaction, a connection. That and the feeling that I somehow knew Axel already.

"Yeah, well, I . . . I grew up in a hurry."

He let go. I took a sip of my tea, just to have something to do with my hand.

The mug quoted *Hamlet* in purple Elizabethan-type print: "To be, or not to be: that is the question."

Uplifting mug.

"I promise I'll be good, okay?" I said it a touch snottily.

I didn't like being told what to do. Especially when it made sense.

"What were you looking for?"

"Huh?" I'd been checking out his weird salt and pepper shakers.

"Is this supposed to be Julius Caesar or something?" I fingered the white one in a toga with a wreath in his hair.

"Yeah, and the pepper's Brutus. Corny, I know. They were a gift."

"Was this mug a gift, too?"

"No, I bought that."

He asked again, "What were you looking through my window for?"

It seemed so stupid now.

"I heard a cello playing. This was the second night. And when I saw your light on . . . I thought it might be coming from here."

"It was."

"It was?"

"Yeah, it was me playing. Why are you surprised?"

"I don't know. . . . I guess you don't look like a cellist."

He sank his head into his hands, elbows on the table.

"What does a cellist look like?"

"Short hair, suit type of guy."

He considered that. "Well, I do own a suit."

His eyebrows creased in thought. "I think I left it back at the town house, though."

"You look more like . . . like a rock star."

He leaned back and gave me a tired look.

"Yeah, yeah. I know. I've heard it all before. Let's not bring Mr. Morrison into this conversation, okay? We'll let the dead stay dead."

"Okay, sure," I said. "It's just that I'm really into Jim. He's kind of like . . ." I looked into my tea, embarrassed. "He's kind of like my only friend."

"That must make for some exciting conversations," Axel said.

I couldn't help but laugh.

"Hey, I made you smile. What do you know, I'm good for something."

He took a shot to celebrate and slammed the glass down.

"I'm sure you're good for more than that."

He shrugged, like he wasn't sure at all.

"I'm making that my mission."

"Excuse me?"

"I'm making it my mission to keep a smile on your face."

This guy was loco.

"Good luck with that."

Before, he wouldn't look at me. Now, I couldn't break away from his stare.

"Why do you care if I smile or not?"

Axel passed his shot glass back and forth a few times between his hands.

"I feel like we're kind of the same."

Suddenly, he sounded dead sober.

"There's this . . . kindred spirit thing going between us. You feel it?"

I'd felt it the moment I saw him. That, more than anything, had been what had sent me running. Who could stand still for a jolt like that? Now it sizzled, this current running through me. But admit to it . . . ?

I leaned back, shifting my shoulders and trying to relax the knot in the back of my neck. It made me uneasy, being kindred spirits with a manic-depressive nut job.

But his eyes were relentless, and I couldn't deny it.

"Yes," I finally replied.

"Well, I . . . I don't want to see you lose your chance."

"To do what?"

"To enjoy life . . . to walk around with a smile."

"Are you saying that you have?"

He stretched his arms out and cracked his knuckles, staring at them.

"Yeah, maybe I am."

Good lord, his mood swings were making me dizzy. Axel was eighteen, handsome, and rich. *What the hell was his problem?*

"I think you'd better lay off *Hamlet* for a while," I said. "And vodka, too."

"The play's the thing," he whispered.

I didn't know how to respond to that, so I didn't.

He snapped out of his trance and looked at me with a sly, drunken smile. "Here's the deal. If you'd like to hang with someone who's actually breathing, I'm available. You're the first person I've felt inclined to talk to in a long time. But no more comparisons to Jim Morrison. I have enough of my own shit without dealing with his."

He held out his hand.

"Can you handle that?"

I shook it.

"I can handle that."

The real question seemed to be, *What was it HE couldn't handle?*

✠

Axel could certainly hold a conversation drunk.

We talked for a long time, about books, mostly. I'd turned a decent number of pages in my life, but he'd read me under the table.

Shakespeare was his favorite. He had the entire collection, leather-bound.

Axel said that Shakespeare had explored every emotion—and that he'd said everything there was to say. According to Axel, everything after Shakespeare was regurgitation. Poetic rehashing.

"You know," I said, "I've always thought they should use Lady Macbeth's 'out damned spot' line in a commercial for a laundry stain remover."

Axel considered that. "Hmm. Or for a carpet cleaner ad, maybe."

I glanced out the window, and my eyes practically bulged out of my head. The sun was rising!

"Oh my God, my aunt's gonna freak!"

I jumped up and looked frantically for the sneakers I'd kicked off. I only found one.

"I gotta run."

Clutching my footwear, I rushed up the steps and out the hatchway. Axel's head popped out after me.

"Hey, Cinderella, catch."

He chucked my other sneaker at me.

"No more wandering around in the dark. You want my phone number?"

"I don't have a phone."

"Then just fluff up your pillow, go back to sleep, and see me in the morning."

"I don't have a pillow."

"You don't have a pillow?" he repeated. "Wait a sec."

He dropped below, then reappeared a few moments later.

"Here," he said, chucking me a pillow in a navy blue case.

I pawed into the feathers, pressed them against my chest.

"Thanks."

I climbed down the ladder to the dock.

It sure beat the way I'd come up.

Light My Fire

I ran across the dock toward the barge. It didn't take long to regret not stopping to slip my sneakers on. The pads of my feet scraped over rough, splintery wood, and I felt the pinch of entrance wounds.

My toes curled against each ladder rung as I climbed, sneakers tucked under one arm, pillow tucked under the other. I lifted the iron latch and pulled the heavy door. Inside, a violin played. I was too late.

The music stopped at the door's creaking. My turn to face the music.

"Willow? I thought you were asleep on the couch."

Aunt Agatha noticed the sneakers and pillow. Then she focused her eyes on me: "What's going on?"

"I . . . um . . ." *Hmmm, this didn't look good, did it?* "I couldn't sleep, so I went on an expedition."

Aunt Agatha used to pick me up on Saturdays and take me out on what she called "expeditions." From going to the museum to picking up baloney at the deli, everything was an exploration, an adventure to her. Like I said, it's all in how you look at things.

She stared at me, wordless. *Not a good sign.*

I shifted my filthy feet.

"I was on the back deck, and I heard music."

Still nothing but a stare. *Freaky.*

I went on: "It sounded like a cello."

"A cello?"

I knew that would grab her.

"Yeah, so I saw a light on in a boat and went on an expedition to see if the cello player was in there."

And I nearly got crushed and drowned. What would Lewis and Clark say?

Aunt Agatha continued her newfound grimness. Not one twinkle surfaced.

"I may have been too hasty in granting you carte blanche, Willow. I thought I could trust you not to abuse your freedoms."

Talk about a crushing blow. Now *I* could only stare.

"When I allowed you to come and go as you pleased, I foolishly assumed that it wouldn't be under cover of darkness."

She pointed the head of her violin at me.

"There are myriad reasons why you may *not* wander around the yard at night. You could walk off the edge of a dock, and no one would even hear you. Must I explain further?"

"No, I get it. Actually, Axel gave me the same sp . . . talk." *With a wandering speech pattern.*

"Axel?"

"He's the guy who was playing the cello."

"Someone named Axel was playing the cello?" She scratched her head. "Did he play it well?"

I shrugged. *What did I know about cello playing?*

"Sounded good to me."

"He lives here?"

"Yeah. On the sailboat *Perchance to Dream*."

Her eyebrows raised.

"Do you mean that hippie boy?"

"Yeah."

"Amazing!" She laughed. "Just when I thought there were no more surprises to be found. Life's a miracle, is it not?"

I shrugged again. *If she said so*.

"And the pillow?"

"Axel gave it to me when he heard I didn't have one. He threw it to me when I was leaving. Really."

I followed her gaze to my toes.

"I lost track of time when we were talking . . . about books."

That got her. She liked books almost as much as instruments.

"And when I saw the sun rising, I ran out without my sneakers on."

She shifted in her chair.

"I don't consider what you did an expedition. It was more like an attempt at suicide. I don't want you roaming the yard at night again. It's fenced in for a reason—to keep trouble out. Don't . . . "

"Go looking for it inside," I finished. "Yeah, I got that. Axel said the same thing."

"Did he?" She smiled broadly.

"Invite that boy over. I'd love to play duets."

I figured I owed it to Aunt Agatha to put in some hard labor, so instead of going to sleep, I washed up and got changed. My feet were riddled with splinters. I'd heard somewhere that you were supposed to let them work themselves out. Sounded better than picking at my skin with tweezers. I put on two pairs of socks to make walking a little less painful.

Oy, I was a wreck.

I was scraping away at wood strips when, to my indescribable joy, Craig sauntered in. I couldn't help noticing his tight muscle shirt. *God, I needed to poke my eyes out with a mahogany strip.*

Then he opened his mouth: "Yo."

"Yo." I could play that game.

"Good morning, Craig," Aunt Agatha sang. "Dear hearts, I have to make some phone calls. I'll be back in about an hour."

My heart sank in direct proportion to the broadening of Craig's smile.

"No problemo, Aggie," he said, with a wink at me.

I thought about heading out, but I'd have to deal with this guy sooner or later. Might as well be when I was operating on zero sleep and standing on throbbing feet. The day was already totaled.

"Toodle-oo, chums," Aunt Agatha called as she pushed through the door.

She couldn't have been more than two steps out when he moved in right next to me, exuding lust like a caveman.

"I been thinkin' 'bout cha."

He should've been thinking about grammar.

I took two steps back and grabbed a piece of wood.

"We've got a lot of work to do." *The understatement of the year.*

He lowered his sunglasses and seemed to study me—if he had the brain capacity to study anything.

"Why ya scared a me?"

I held the long strip across my chest.

"I'm not scared. I'm just busy. No time to chat."

"You one a doze goody-goodies?"

He came close again and stroked my cheek, slowly. He may've been a moron, but he sure wasn't bad at touching.

My mahogany shook in my hands, but I didn't move away.

He smiled. "Ya want me ta teach ya ta be bad?"

He really needed to learn some dialogue. Still, I let him touch me again. *Was I desperate or what?*

My heart pounded so hard I thought it would break down. His face came closer, in slow motion.

His lips pressed on mine, and I allowed it.

His hands gripped my back, pulling me tight against him. Still, I allowed it.

I felt terrified. I felt repulsed. But more than anything, I felt a blinding need.

His hands slipped under my shirt, against my skin. I wanted him to stop; I wanted him to go on. . . .

He slipped his tongue in my mouth. It slid around. A thick, slimy slug. Uggh!

The spell broke. I shoved the wood I was still clutching against his chest, pushing him away.

"Whatsamatta?"

"Nothing. I just—I just didn't sleep much. I'm tired."

"Yeah?" He ran his finger down my cheek again, sending a chill through me. "Ya let me know when you're not tired, 'kay?"

I stared at him, knowing I should say something scathing.

"'Kay." *Nice going.*

I went back to stripping my wood. But my mind kept going back to the other kind of stripping I'd almost done.

It was all wrong with Craig. Wrong, wrong, wrong.

And yet . . . he did have a nice touch.

Not that I had anything to compare it to.

Aunt Agatha came back, wearing a frown.

"Hello, chums," she said, at half her usual pitch.

"What's wrong?" I paused my scraper halfway down a strip.

"Oh . . . I . . . I just never imagined it would be this hard." She sank into her practicing chair and leaned back with a heavy sigh.

"What? Fixing up the place?"

"No, no. Not that. It's what I have no control over that upsets me. Finding a berth for the barge." She looked out into the water. "What good is a concert barge with no place to dock?"

You'd think she'd have worked all this out beforehand.

"So you were calling about berths?"

"My dear, I've been calling about berths for months. I'm almost out of places to call. No one's interested in a concert barge. You should hear what they say!"

I could just imagine.

"So what are you going to do?" I asked.

She looked at me and smiled.

"Don't worry about me, love. I may be stalled, but I'm not giving up. Sometimes it just takes me a few seconds to restart my engine."

"Hey, good one," Craig said. *It figured he'd like the car reference, stereotype that he was.*

"Thank you, dear heart," she told him.

To me, she said, "There's something else, love. I'm afraid I'll have to go back to work, starting tomorrow."

Aunt Agatha played in the orchestra pit in Broadway shows. She despised playing the same mindless pieces night after night. She could actually play from memory and read a book at the same time.

"I thought you were taking the summer off," I said.

"Yes, but apparently my fill-in just quit. Go figure." She waved her arms up. "If I don't go back, they'll replace me permanently."

This wasn't good at all. It meant way too much alone time for Craig and me.

"Don't worry, dear heart. There are only two matinees a week, and the rest of the performances are in the evenings. We'll be able to get our work done without much interference. And you prefer to eat supper alone, anyway. Just let me know what you want to eat, and I'll make sure it's here."

She rose and took my hand. "We'll get by."

I glanced over at Craig, who seemed to be hard at work, hammering wood to the wall. Only two matinees, and one was probably Sunday. He wouldn't be working on a Sunday anyway. When she went to the other matinee, I could just leave.

That's it. I'd leave.

Aunt Agatha's back was turned now as she got to work on staining.

Craig gave me a lewd half smile.

God, I hoped I'd leave.

Confessions

By the end of the day, I was ready to scrape at my skin with tweezers. My feet burned like I'd walked over hot coals.

I peeled off my socks and showed Aunt Agatha. She said I needed to soak them in Epsom salts so the splinters would work themselves out.

She set me up on the couch with my feet in an aluminum paint pan filled with warm water and the Epsom salts and with a pair of tweezers at my side. I was amazed she had the salts, but apparently foot soaking was one luxury she allowed herself. Thankfully, the salted water put out the fire under my soles.

She'd also insisted on leaving me linguine, saying I needed a real meal. It was still in the blackened pot she'd cooked it in, on the hot plate. Aunt Agatha believed in eating right from the pot.

While I sat and soaked, the linguine sat and soaked, too—in the oil Aunt Agatha had globbed onto it and stirred. The fat count in that pot had to be in the high hundreds. I crunched on a carrot and thought of the Brady family.

Real meals always made me think of them. They were on this TV show I watched every night at seven, "The Brady Bunch." It was on Channel 5, a station that showed old sitcoms.

Tuning into *The Brady Bunch* was like studying a foreign culture: Dad was always hard at work, supporting the family, and yet he came home every single night, just in time for supper. Mom was a homemaker, pretty much only leaving the house on errands. Alice was the maid and cook, which kind of makes me wonder what Mom actually did all day. Somehow, she seemed pretty busy.

The Bradys had six kids whose problems were a total joke, like breaking Mom's favorite vase and trying to cover it up or not wanting to share a room anymore.

I would have loved those problems.

And the best part was that their problems were always solved by the end of every episode. Life was restored to a bed of roses in thirty minutes, minus commercials. You can't beat that.

My mom was pretty much everything Mrs. Brady was not.

My mom didn't have a favorite vase to break. She was too busy piling up unread newspapers all over the place. There wasn't a chair or table without them.

My mom never cleaned or cooked, nor did she hire a housekeeper to do it. In fact, my mom never even showed up for dinner. Eight o'clock would've been early for her. A real treat for me.

When I lived with Mom, I sat on my newspapers and watched Alice clean. I ate my canned soup and watched the

Bradys seated around the dinner table, discussing their day and passing the potatoes.

But on the barge, I had no TV. So, three carrots later, I moved the linguine to the floor and slipped my headphones on. I dozed off, still sitting up and still soaking my feet, during a long instrumental part of a Doors song. Before I fell asleep, my last thought was, *What on earth did Jim do during those parts at concerts? He didn't play an instrument. The music wasn't danceable. Did he just stand there looking sexy? Hmmm . . .*

I woke up some time later, with my head arched back. My neck had an awful cramp.

I decided to check my feet. Darned if the splinters weren't poking out a bit—most of them, anyway. I plucked them out, one by one.

It would be great if you could squeeze the tweezers and pluck the problems out of your life.

My feet were still sore, but the severe pain was gone. I padded them up with the same two pairs of socks, then slid my sneakers on. I got up and took the pot of linguine out to the back deck, held it over the water and dumped it. Splash! The lump of twisted strands sunk like a lead weight.

"Hey!" someone called in a raised whisper.

I jumped, and fought back a scream.

"Willow!"

I peeked over the edge of the deck and saw Axel.

"You always go prowling around at one a.m.?" I asked.

"Actually, it's a quarter to ten," he said, checking his watch. "Close, though."

Boy, I needed a clock. I was becoming more and more removed from time as the world knew it.

"What's up?" I asked.

"Just felt like talking. Thought maybe you'd feel like it, too."

Oh, yeah. I did.

"Come up the ladder at the other end," I told him. "I'll meet you there."

I headed across the barge to the front door, stopping at the couch to drop off the empty pot.

Again, I had to feel my way through the dark patch of the room—didn't want to step on any protruding nails. Or wake Aunt Agatha up. At last, I made it out the front door.

"Sorry I took so long. It's like running an obstacle course in there," I said.

"Really?"

"Yeah, go ahead—take a peek."

I opened the door, and he stared inside.

"Yikes."

"And you can't even see half of it in the dark. I'm telling you, I don't see how this place is ever going to be finished."

I closed the door again.

Axel leaned against the wall. "What's it going to be?"

I sat on a metal stump, just like the one I'd stubbed my toe on, there on the back deck. Aunt Agatha said it was used to wrap rope around and to attach the barge to tugboats.

"It's supposed to be a classical music concert hall— for chamber music. That's music for a small group of musicians, as opposed to an orchestra."

"Yeah, I know." He played an imaginary bow across his chest. "The cello, remember?"

"Oh, yeah. Sorry. I'm just used to explaining it to people."

"So how'd your aunt come up with this idea?"

"Strangely enough, it's because of me. When I was born, Aunt Agatha decided she wanted a haven for me—those were her words. God, this sounds corny. Anyway, she wanted a place for me—and the rest of the world—to hear beautiful music performed as it was meant to be. In a place where you could see the musicians' faces as they played. A place for the soul and the spirit. Yeesh, I've got the whole lecture memorized."

"Sounds great."

"Yeah, well, anything can sound good in theory. But when it comes time to actually doing it . . ."

"So you don't think the barge is gonna work out?"

"You see what needs to be done. I guess it's possible. But she's got a bigger problem. She can't find a place to dock it in New York City."

"That stinks."

"Yes, it does."

What didn't stink was this night. Axel seemed to have stabilized. He wasn't shy; he wasn't overbearing. And he wasn't drunk.

"Anyway, it's time for true confessions," I said. "I need to know: how'd you wind up in this boatyard of your own free will?"

Axel laughed. "I just needed to get away and chill for

a while, and I've always liked the water. I told my dad I wanted to take some time off before college."

He paused, and the smile left his face. "He didn't have a problem with it. He gave me one of his boats. I changed its name, because *Boardroom Antics* didn't work for me— and off I went."

Interesting.

"How much time you taking off?"

"Jury's still out on that."

Okay.

"So, you have any brothers or sisters?"

"Three brothers: Wade, Wesley, and Will."

"Are you close with them?"

"Ha. Like anyone could be close with those banana Republicans."

"I take it they're the short hair, dark suit types?"

"Yeah, but to blow your theory again, not one of them plays the cello. They're only interested in playing the stock market."

Something about the name thing seemed off.

"How did Wade, Wesley, and Will wind up with a brother called Axel?"

"They're my half brothers. They're all a lot older than I am. Thirty-five, thirty-two, and thirty. Their mom died 'bout twenty years ago. Cancer."

"Sorry to hear that."

Axel shrugged.

"And what about your mom?" I asked.

"She was Dad's secretary—or one of them. He was bonking them all, I imagine, but the condom broke in her."

71

"Wow."

"Well, you asked. Tell you the truth, she probably made a hole in it. And then—there I was."

You couldn't accuse Axel of holding anything back.

He continued, "Dad married Mom. It wouldn't do for a little bastard to be running around, even though I suspect he's always thought of me that way anyway. I'm told he wanted me named after a philosopher. But Mom didn't want to name her son Aristotle or Socrates. He said she could pick, but it had to be a name having to do with philosophy."

"I never heard of any philosopher named Axel," I said.

"No, but it's kind of funny what she did. She looked up philosophy in the thesaurus and found the synonym *axiology*. So she named me Axel for short. Needless to say, Dad wasn't thrilled. Tricked again, by a bimbo."

"That's not a nice way to talk about your mother."

Axel shrugged. "I suppose I should be grateful that my name's not Phil." He locked his fingers together and stared down at them.

"Seriously, I think my name was just another reason for my dad to hate me."

"I'm sure your father doesn't hate you."

Axel looked up. "Yeah? You know him, huh?"

"Well, no. . . ."

"Then you'll have to trust me on that. One thing's for sure: Dad and my so-called brothers didn't shed any tears when I sailed off into the sunset."

"So, has being named after philosophy itself compelled you to spout out any words of wisdom?"

Axel reflected for a moment and said, "Life sucks."

And there you have it.

"Where's your mom now?" I asked him.

"Gone."

"Gone?"

Axel nodded.

"Gone. She split. Took off with the gardener, a real class act named Eddie Cuccioni, Junior."

"Jeez, I'm really sorry."

He shrugged.

"Tell you the truth, I'm not a big fan of foliage. Kind of makes me think of them. That's why I like it around here. No flowers anywhere."

"That's terrible," I said.

Axel shrugged again.

"There *are* worse things than that in the world."

He swiped his hands together, like he was done with the subject.

"Okay, your turn. Tell me about your rotten childhood," he said.

"How do you know I had a rotten childhood?"

"You exude eau de rotten childhood. You reek of it. What do you think drew me to you to begin with? Your misery lures me."

"You sure know how to compliment a girl."

He shrugged yet again. It was getting to be his all-purpose response.

I told him about the loneliness. About getting off the school bus and heading down the block, walking past all the neat, orderly houses to our haunted-looking one.

It was something the Addams family would've been happy in. Paint was peeling off in chunks; the doorknob was taped up to try and keep it from falling off in your hand. You had to practically body-slam the door to get it to open, and we had this huge, unruly hedge that the town board always wrote to complain about.

I told him about having to fend for myself until Mom came home at around nine at night, if not later, and I told him about all the newspapers, the years and years of *The New York Times* Mom was saving until she had time to read them.

How Axel felt about flowers, that's how I felt about newsprint.

And I told him about how Mom had different voices. How she could be a little girl sometimes, soft and questioning. I'd have to explain everything to her, like I was the grown-up. Then there was the mad voice, which was attacking, blaming, and vicious. Times like that, she wouldn't even say good morning. Instead, she'd just hurl anger at me, like rocks.

I guess Axel couldn't accuse me of holding back, either.

"Hmmm," Axel said when I'd finished. "I guess we could open a chapter of Dysfunctions Are Us, huh?"

"Yeah, I guess we could."

"But you haven't explained how you wound up here this summer. Doesn't seem like you volunteered for the job."

"Mom found herself a boyfriend. A plumber she called to fix a leak a few months ago. God, it's like a bad movie."

"Yeah, a bad porno movie."

"I wouldn't know about that," I said. "Anyway, he made himself right at home. So he was in, and I was out."

"What's gonna happen in the fall?"

I didn't know what was going to happen to me in the fall. Maybe Mom would decide she didn't want me back. Maybe she'd run off with Steve to Paris.

What if I had to stay on the barge always? With no bed, no shower, no TV?

"You got any extra room on that boat?"

He laughed. But I wasn't kidding.

He got up. "It's late now. I'd better go."

That reminded me: "Tomorrow, I need to get a clock somehow."

"This should take care of it," Axel said, handing me a small silver object. It was a flip-top cell phone. "I had it delivered today. Look, it has the time on it—and the date. So you can count down each day you serve."

"Axel, why . . . ?"

"I could see you were scared here. Now you know you can call 911 if you need to. And if it's not an emergency, you can call me." He took the phone and flipped it open. He hit "Phonebook." The name "Axel" appeared. "You're the first one to get my number besides the Chinese restaurant."

"Your family doesn't have your phone number?"

"I told you, I didn't feel like talking to anyone."

"What if there's an emergency?"

"What kind of emergency? The dry cleaner didn't press Wesley's suits to his expectations?" He laughed, but it seemed forced. "They wouldn't look to me for help, and I sure as hell wouldn't call them. Anyway, I'm beyond help."

"I don't understand. . . ."

"At least you've got a shot at salvation." *Salvation? He was talking crazy again. What, did he think he was Jesus Christ or something?*

I must have given him a weird look, because he apologized. "I didn't mean to say it like that. I just meant, now you don't have to be lonely anymore."

If only it were that easy.

Break on Through

The barge seemed more bearable with a friend to talk to. Aunt Agatha left for the theater at five o'clock every night, and Axel came by at six. I told him to come earlier sometime and meet Aunt Agatha, but so far he hadn't wanted to. I said she'd invited him to play duets, but he didn't want to do that, either. He said he didn't play well with others.

Axel usually stayed until about eleven o'clock. We sat on the deck and stared into the water, talking about anything that came into our heads.

Axel also brought me a pile of books, to keep me from going nuts alone on the barge. He tried to give me Shakespeare, but I told him I was getting enough of the Bard from him already. I asked for Jane Austen and the Brontë sisters.

During the day, I tried my best to help Aunt Agatha. And I had to admit, we were making some progress. One-third of a wall was now covered in mahogany, and it looked great—and interesting, too. The strips varied in length and shades of brown, giving the overall effect of a giant wooden jigsaw puzzle, just like Aunt Agatha had promised. Craig wasn't so bad with a saw and hammer. Too bad someone couldn't hammer some grammar into him.

Of course, the rest of the huge chamber continued to be a dismal wreck. At the rate we were going, I calculated that the work would probably be done in time to celebrate my thirtieth birthday.

On Wednesdays and Sundays, Aunt Agatha left for the theater at noon. Sundays, Axel came to keep me company, and I put him to work, too. On Wednesdays, Craig was there, so I wasn't.

One Wednesday, three weeks after Aunt Agatha went back to work, I followed her down the dock to the parking lot.

"Where are you off to, love?" She knew I never stayed on the barge with Craig. I'd told her I didn't enjoy trying to hold an intelligent conversation with him, and she'd laughed and said that she understood.

"I don't know . . . probably Axel's."

"You see so much of him."

"Yeah?"

"I'd like to meet this young man you spend so much time with."

"I told him. It's just . . . he's shy, I guess."

But I really wasn't sure why Axel avoided Aunt Agatha.

"Strange," Aunt Agatha said as we reached her car—an old, battered Volkswagen Beetle. "But what in life isn't strange?"

Not much.

Certainly not Aunt Agatha's car. The word *battered*

didn't even begin to describe it. Its powder blue body probably had more dents than its odometer had miles. The front bumper was tied to the car with thick orange rope. But the worst thing, in my opinion, was that the upper half of the passenger seat was totally gone. She'd removed it to make room for the long pieces of wood paneling for the barge that she'd transported herself, one stack at a time. (Apparently, Aunt Agatha hadn't heard of U-Haul.) And only the bottom of the rear seat remained. Besides that, the wooden boards had also poked a rather large hole through the passenger floor.

I found this out when she took me out one morning to buy groceries.

"Hang on, love!" she shouted above the broken muffler whenever she had to make a turn. I had to clamp my hands down on what was left of my seat and prop my feet against the dashboard, all the while wondering what I'd done to deserve this.

Luckily, I didn't need to travel much with Aunt Agatha.

As I walked her to her car, she looked around and frowned. Her car was parked in a legitimate spot near the barge at the boatyard, but someone had parked a red Oldsmobile right behind her, boxing her in so she couldn't back out from the space.

"How will I get to work?" she asked, sounding a little desperate.

A tall, burly, bearded guy walking by overheard her and asked, "Need some help, ma'am?"

"I don't know how you can help me, dear heart, unless you can lift my car out of there."

"Be right back," the man said, then headed off behind some scaffolded boats. He returned quickly with three equally tall, burly men.

"We need to rescue this lady's car," the bearded guy told his friends, pointing to the blocked-in VW.

The four men each bent down at a corner of the car. Then they lifted it together, effortlessly, kicking through pebbles as they carried it right up and over the offending Olds.

Then they set it down—crrrunnnccchhh—in the gravel.

"Dear hearts, how will I ever repay you?" Aunt Agatha asked, shaking their hands.

"That's what we do around here, ma'am. We help each other out," said the bearded guy. The other three nodded.

"I'll remember that," said Aunt Agatha. She gave me a kiss and popped into her VW. The engine roared. "Toodle-oo, chums!" she yelled, waving to us as she zoomed away, her muffler puffing out a black cloud in her wake.

"Let's go for a walk," I suggested to Axel.

"Not much room to walk around here without banging into boats on stilts," he said. We were sitting in his galley, as usual, and I was getting antsy. I wanted to roam.

"No, I mean, let's walk around the neighborhood."

Axel leaned forward, stretching his arms across the table almost like he was going to grab me. "No way. For-get it," he said.

"Oh, come on. Don't you want some exercise?"

"Not that badly." He gave me that look. "Seriously, Willow. Not a good idea."

Of course, this made me want to go even more. As Aunt Agatha always said, opposition breeds opposition.

"I wasn't asking for your permission. If you don't want to go, I'll go without you."

"Oh, no, you won't." His voice had that firmness to it now that made me determined.

"Watch me," I said.

I got up, headed up the ladder to the deck, then down the ladder to the dock, all without looking back. I went up the dock, through the parking lot, to the gate. I wondered if he was behind me, but I refused to look back and check.

The minute I stepped through the gate into the street, I regretted my hasty decision. But I couldn't turn back. I mean, I could've. But I wouldn't let myself. I was being stubborn—very stubborn.

I decided I'd circle a few blocks and stay out for only about fifteen minutes. That'd be enough to make my point to Axel.

I walked along, squinting in the strong, hot sun. Sweat formed under my bangs and on the back of my neck under my ponytail.

The neighboring houses were so sad. They looked like they'd never been inviting, and now time had really done them in. Their paint was faded or missing in patches, shingles were hanging off at an angle or gone, and the top layers of roof shingles were ripped off, leaving their black undercoating exposed. And those were the good ones—the houses in better shape.

Others, in worse shape, had broken steps, broken porches, or boarded-up windows. In the entrance to one little green cement house, a sheet hung instead of a front door. You had to guess there were a whole lot of broken lives to go along with those messed-up houses.

There weren't many people around. Probably at the beach—the one escape they had in this heat. I wasn't sure if this was good or bad, that I was pretty much alone. But I was leaning toward bad. After all, there's safety in numbers, and I wasn't feeling so safe.

Once in a while, I could see a figure leaning in a doorway.

And then, under the awning of a bodega blaring Spanish music, two guys in sunglasses sat on turned-over boxes, drinking malt liquor.

One of them eyed me.

Oh, boy.

I walked faster.

I turned another corner. Halfway down the street, two Latino guys blocked the way. I tried to go around them, but one of them stepped right in front of me, blocking me again. He had a scrawny body and a scrawny black moustache, also a goatee. His hair was short and slicked back. He wore a gold chain and a cross that looked like they weighed twice as much as he did.

"Hey, baby." He reached out and touched my hand.

Excuse me? I flinched, pulled my hand back.

"Whatsmatta, baby?" he cooed at me, revealing a gold tooth. He reached for me again, but I stepped back.

I just stared at him, speechless. I never thought anyone would approach me so directly like this.

"What's a looker like you doin' slumming round here? You looking for me?" He moved closer again. I felt his body heat, and I wanted to vomit.

I stared at him a moment longer. Then a voice inside me said, *Go. Get out of here, now!*

I turned, willing my feet to run without seeing clearly where I was going.

I ran in the direction I'd come from.

And I ran straight into someone else.

"Happy now?" he asked. It was Axel.

I looked up at him. His face kind of swirled around me. Everything was so tense, hot, and blurry that I just couldn't focus.

He grabbed my arm, pulling me forward. Walking quickly, he hauled me all the way back to the boatyard. In my neighborhood, someone would have called the cops if someone had done that. But here, nobody batted an eye.

By the time we got back, I was thinking and seeing clearly again. My heart was pounding hard. I wanted to press my hands against it to hold it in.

Inside the gate, Axel released his grip on me.

"What am I going to do with you?" he asked, sounding disgusted and waving his hands in my face.

"Who said you have to do anything?" I leaned back into the fence, folding my arms tight against my chest to get some relief. "I'm not your problem, so don't worry about me."

He huffed, "I don't get you, Willow. Can't you see when you're in over your head?"

Sure. But seeing it and doing something about it are two different things.

I really was grateful he'd followed me. But damned if I was going to let him know it.

"Guess what, buddy. You left your shining armor back home."

"You can talk tough, Willow, but I know you're glad I was there." He gave me another one of his deep looks. "I *know* you're glad."

Claustrophobic

Axel didn't show up later, and I didn't care. I'd walked away from him in the driveway without even a look back.

Who needed him, anyway?

I sprawled on the couch and opened *Wuthering Heights* to page 98, where I'd left off earlier. Midway down the third page, the words blurred. The book thumped on the floor in the distance, like someone else had dropped it.

My eyes open and try to focus, but there's nothing to see. It's dark. So dark. Where am I?

I'm lying with my head on my arm. The pulse beating through my arm distracts me and makes it hard to think. I lift my head and roll onto my stomach.

I spread my hands, feel all around where I'm lying. There's nothing but floor.

And it's dark. So dark.

I scramble to my feet and go. But which way? I don't know. Just out. I want out of this darkness.

I bang into a wall. Oh my God, oh my God!

I go the other way. I smash into another wall. Oh my God, oh my God!

Everywhere, there are walls. I'm in a box. I'm in a box.

There's no sound except for my heartbeat, racing faster and faster. I'm locked in a box of darkness. Let me out! Let me out!

I throw myself against a wall and bang, bang, bang with my hands.

"Help!"

No one comes.

I'm in a box of darkness, and no one's coming.

I punch into the wall. Again, again. I kick, kick, kick. My hands and feet throb, but the pain can't keep up with my terror.

"Help me!" I shout, and then choke down saliva and salt.

I'm shaking, shaking. I collapse to the floor, curling into a ball.

I'm in a box of darkness, and no one's coming.

I'm in a box of darkness, and no one's coming.

I'm in a box of darkness, and no one's coming.

I'm going to die in here.

My eyes popped open. *Where am I?*

I jumped up and off the couch. I looked around; I could see. I could actually see.

It's okay, it's okay. I know where I am.

But oh my God, I can't be alone.

Please, I can't be alone.

The phone. *In my suitcase. In the side pocket.*

Zzzzip. I dug in, feeling papers, the iPod . . . then, at the bottom, I finally grabbed it.

8:32 p.m.

I grabbed open the top and tried to remember what to do to call him.

What do I do? What do I do?

"Menu," the button in the middle. "Menu," that was it.

Beep. The menu gave me more choices.

Just dial the damn number!

Phonebook. I hit "Phonebook."

Beep.

Axel. It said "Axel."

I hit "Send."

It said "Calling Axel."

Ring, ring.

It said "Connected with Axel."

"I guess you're over your fit," he said.

"Come here," I pleaded, breathing the words out hard.

"What's the matter?"

"Please."

"I'll be right there."

From the front deck, I watched him. Bathed in yellow from the dim mounted lights, he hurried across the dock toward me.

87

I lost sight of him as he mounted the ladder. Finally, I saw the top of his head, then the rest of him. He hauled himself onto the deck and came to me. He held me, and I threw my arms around him, hung on tight, pressing my head against his cotton shirt. He was so warm. I felt safe with his arms covering me and protecting me.

My heartbeat synchronized with his strong, steady beat. I stopped trembling, relieved at having him so close.

Axel just held me, without asking any questions. He was just there for me. Finally, someone was there for me, without making any demands at all.

❈

"Thanks," I said, releasing him from my death grip.

"For what?"

"For coming."

"It's my job, remember?"

"I thought your job was to make me smile."

"Well, you certainly weren't going to smile in the middle of a panic attack. I had to get you through it."

We sat outside on the barge's deck with our backs against the wall and stared at the stars. Another beautiful night.

After a while, he finally asked, "Want to talk about it?"

I drew in a deep breath and let it out. "I have this nightmare sometimes. It used to be all the time; now, not so much. Not for a while, anyway. That's probably why I freaked like that." I turned to him. "You think I'm crazy, huh? All this, over a nightmare."

"I don't think you're crazy." He took my hand. "Tell me. What happens in the dream?"

"I'm trapped in a pitch black box. I can't see anything." I shuddered. "I scream, I bang, I kick, but no one comes to help me. I just curl up and die."

"You die in your dream?"

"Well, no. I just know that I'm going to die. I can feel it. Then I wake up."

"I'm sorry. I wish I could do something about it."

"It just sucks being alone when . . . when I'm scared."

"I know."

"But you *choose* to be alone."

"There was no one there for me at home. The house staff didn't care about me. My brothers didn't care about me. My dad didn't even care about me. Might as well be alone on my own terms."

Like me, at Christmas.

"My mom always leaves me alone on Christmas Eve," I told him. "She waits until that night to go shopping. It's like Christmas completely slips her mind until the twenty-fourth. She doesn't even buy a tree until then. So I always end up sitting in front of the TV, watching other families do stuff, deck the halls and whatever."

"What about your aunt?"

"Aw, she doesn't do the holiday thing. She just treats it like any other time of year."

"Wouldn't she come if you asked her?"

"I don't know. I never thought of asking her."

"You should."

Axel was so sweet. I felt so much better, so secure with him there.

I was struck with a crazy impulse. I kissed his cheek. "Make love to me."

"What?"

"Make love to me."

"Why would you go and say something like that?" His voice was sharp.

"We're two lonely, miserable people. We could make each other feel better. . . . "

"And when we finished, we'd still be two lonely, miserable people. Sex isn't a band-aid for our wounds."

"I want to be close to you."

"You *are* close to me. I've told you stuff no one knows. Hell, I've never even gotten off my boat for anyone else."

He got up and paced, going from one side of the deck to the other. Back and forth, back and forth.

"Why do you want to have sex so badly? You're fifteen. You're still a goddamn kid."

"Why *don't* you want to have sex? You're an eighteen-year-old guy. Isn't it, like, something you want to do all the time?"

Axel didn't answer. Just paced faster, like a cougar I watched one time at the zoo.

I looked down. "Am I that ugly?"

He stopped pacing and stooped by me. "Willow, you're beautiful." He lifted my chin and forced me to look at him. "You're so beautiful that I couldn't hurt you."

Beautiful, my butt. "How is sex gonna hurt me?"

"You're not ready for it. It'd change you forever. And . . . you'd hate me."

"No way."

"One day, when you understood what I'd done—when it dawned on you, then you'd hate me. You're fifteen. There's a reason why they call you underage."

He brushed my bangs aside and pecked my forehead. "Wait."

Whatever. I knew all his words were bullshit. I knew the real reason he'd rejected me. It was because I was a dog. A fat beast. An obese hound.

He sat down again.

"You understand, right?"

"Yeah. I understand."

Suddenly, a voice came out of the night: "Well, well. Who do we have here? Could it be the mysterious Axel?"

Aunt Agatha was back early.

Open Wounds 12

"I didn't mean to startle you," said Aunt Agatha. "There was a power failure at the theater during intermission, and the show couldn't go on." She didn't seem too broken up about that. "I must say, I didn't complain. I'm utterly exhausted!"

"Hi, Aunt Agatha. Yes, this is Axel," I said. I looked at him, only to find him staring at the goddamn steel deck. We were back to the no eye contact, shy routine.

"Hello, dear heart."

I nudged him. He shot me an anxious look, but then he got up.

"Pleasure to meet you, Ms. Moon," he said, standing and extending his hand.

She took his hand in both of hers and shook it vigorously.

"Welcome home, darling. And it's Agatha. Only tax collectors and solicitors call me Ms. Moon."

"Okay, Agatha." He shuffled his feet.

Good lord, how could the same guy who'd saved me

from a dangerous situation out on the street, plus rescued me from a panic attack now revert to a nearly mute bundle of nerves, all in the same day? He needed medication or something.

"I like your face, dear heart. It's sincere. And my niece tells me you're a cellist."

"Yes." He looked down again.

"You must come play duets with me. And I won't take no for an answer."

"Oh, I don't think so. . . ."

"I have the sheet music for Beethoven's Duo for Violin and Cello in E-flat Major. You know, the one he subtitled in the manuscript 'with two obbligato eyeglasses,' but no one knows why." She made finger circles over her eyes. "Fun, fun!"

Axel stared at her, dumbstruck.

"Come, come. What are the chances of two musicians meeting in a setting like this? We must take advantage of our good fortune."

"I'm not really up to it."

"Pish, posh. Is anyone ever up to anything in life?"

"I need to practice."

"You can practice with me, darling. I'm not God or the devil. I'm not going to judge you or poke you with a pitchfork."

Axel laughed. "Well, when you put it like that. . . . Okay. I'll come."

"Tomorrow morning, then."

"Tomorrow morning?"

"Indeed. Because I'm so tired, I'm forced to employ

the cliché 'There's no time like the present.' It does the job, does it not?"

"Yes, it does. I'll be here." He turned to me. "I'd better get going."

"Dear heart, don't leave on my account. I'm going to bed. You two are young. You can stay up a while longer." She poked Axel in the chest. "As long as you're here at sunrise, mister."

"Sunrise?"

"Sunrise. If you don't get going early, you don't get going at all." Aunt Agatha chuckled and elbowed Axel in the ribs. "I'm out of my mind with fatigue and am able to summon only trite platitudes. The one about the early bird springs to mind. Then there's 'He who snoozes, loses.' Lord, what would Shakespeare say?"

"If it were done when 'tis done, then 'twere well. It were done quickly?" Axel suggested. He seemed to be handling his first Aunt Agatha experience pretty well after all.

"Indeed," Aunt Agatha said. "Macbeth was talking about murder, of course, but practicing the fiddle may certainly be called deadly." She slapped Axel on the back. "I like your style, my boy."

She yanked the door, then paused with it open. "Oh, I almost forgot to tell you about my adventure tonight, on the way to work."

"What happened?" I asked.

"I was stopped at a light. All of a sudden, I saw a tire go rolling across the street and up a telephone pole. It was the darndest thing. Then suddenly, the car flopped— voom! It was *my* tire!"

"What did you do?" asked Axel, looking appalled.

"I walked to a gas station and asked them to come and fix it. Lucky it didn't happen on the Belt Parkway."

"That's true," I said.

❀

"Sorry about that. Aunt Agatha's a bit . . . much," I said after she'd closed the door behind her.

"No, no. I like her. And to think I spent so much energy avoiding her."

"Why did you, anyway?"

"Avoid her?" He shrugged. "I avoid all adults. They're basically all full of shit. But Agatha seems to be on the level."

"That she is."

"Are you okay?" he asked me.

"Yeah, sure. I'm fine now." *Then why did I feel wiped out?*

"You surfed an emotional wave tonight."

"The ride's over, so don't worry about me."

He stared at me, like he was deciding whether I was lying.

But I'm really good at burying things deep. I've had lots of practice.

The yellow light on the dock behind him flickered and died. *Lights out, everyone.*

"I guess I'll go, then," he said softly.

"See ya."

"Good night." He turned toward the ladder.

Watching him go, I felt like a balloon with a leak, deflating slowly. "Axel, wait. . . . I'm . . . I'm sorry about what I said, um, suggested before."

"It's forgotten. Don't sweat it."

"Thanks for coming. I . . . I don't know how else I'd have gotten through that."

"Talk to your aunt. Maybe she can help you."

"I don't think so."

"I would've loved someone like her to talk to." He looked past me at the water.

"It's just not that easy."

"Why not?"

"I don't know. I guess it's because she expects so much from me."

"What's that got to do with it?"

"Nothing. Everything. You saw how she is. Two minutes after you meet her, she's got you playing duets at the crack of dawn. She's like a bulldozer."

"Oh, come on. I don't mind coming."

"But it wouldn't matter to her if you did or you didn't. She'd already decided what was best for you. Imagine living with that all the time."

"She cares, that's all."

"She cares, yes, but too much. I mean, like, when I was little, she taught me violin. If I tell you I hated it, that wouldn't be strong enough. But she . . . she wouldn't let me stop. She pushed and pushed. She even paid me for each line I played—for years."

"Lots of kids have to take music lessons."

"But she's like that with everything. Push, push, push.

But it's not just what to do. She even tells me what to think. She . . . she corrects my thoughts. And if I tell her about a problem, she tells me I'm suffering from ego sickness."

I glanced at the sky. The stars seemed so close. I wished I could just jump aboard one and head off into the galaxy. But instead, I was stuck on Earth, with hurt and resentment gushing out of me like I was an open fire hydrant.

"Lately, she's been a bit better. . . . I think it's because she's so wrapped up in this barge. I . . . I don't want to get her started. She'd probably blame me for my own nightmare and tell me to wipe it out of my head."

"I doubt that. Have you ever really sat down and discussed things with her?"

"No, that's just it. Whenever I start . . . anyway, she . . . she goes into this big philosophical speech . . . and that's that. To her, the problem's solved. Time to move on, get to work."

The tears were flowing again. *Goddamn it. I was such a wuss.*

"Try and talk to her. She might surprise you."

I sucked in a deep breath and blew it out. "Right now, Axel, I don't know if I could handle any more surprises."

13
Duet

Heading back inside, I kicked up a screw or a nail or something. It went sailing, clinking against the steel wall.

I plopped down on the couch, hearing the ringing in my head. The sound of that screw hitting metal jarred the memory of long-ago dinging, back when I was nine.

It was a Saturday. The plan was for my Uncle Sid to teach Mom to drive. I had my doubts about it, because Uncle Sid had tried to do things for Mom before, but he'd never actually been successful. That's because he gets mad at her and leaves.

The problem is that my mom's voice has this hook in it. It's this sharp, jabbing hook that just sticks you, even when someone's doing something nice for her. She needles you and starts a fight. But Uncle Sid, he's not one to take her bait. He'd rather just take off. That's why we don't see him all that often. And that's why it took Mom forever to learn how to drive. But there is one kind of driving that Mom's always been really good at, and that's driving people away.

Anyway, here's what happened when he tried to teach

her how to drive: Mom and Uncle Sid sat in the front of the faded red Volvo Mom inherited from her other brother, Jerry, after he died. It'd been sitting in the driveway for as long as I could remember, and she started it sometimes to keep the battery from going bad or something like that.

I sat buckled up in the back, even though no one told me to. I knew I was supposed to wear the seat belt or maybe I'd get killed. "Seat belts save lives"—that's what they said on TV.

The big plan was that after the driving lesson, we were going to Pancake Cottage. We'd have a nice family breakfast. Almost like the Brady Bunch, except it was my uncle instead of my dad. And the Bradys had home-cooked meals. And if they did go out to eat, you can bet Mr. and Mrs. Brady always told their kids to buckle up.

Uncle Sid groaned. "It's a stick. How can you learn to drive on a stick? It'll take forever."

She said, "Shut up. If it takes forever, then that's too bad." And there was that hook.

They were already yelling, and the car wasn't even started yet. Then she turned the key, and when the engine started running, it was loud! Uncle Sid said maybe it needed a muffler, but Mom said it was just old.

He told her how to back up, but the stick made a really bad noise when she moved it—like someone choking a duck—and then the car stalled. Uncle Sid cursed and told her again how to do it. After, like, thirteen tries, we finally got out of the driveway. I wasn't really bothered by all this because I was reading *The Hardy Boys*, volume 33. I loved those Hardy boys. I loved them more than Nancy Drew.

We were moving now, but I was still reading, trying not to listen to the driving lesson. The car kept stalling; Uncle Sid kept cursing: "Goddamn it!" And Mom kept cursing louder: "Shut the fuck up! How can I concentrate?" This was how she was with everyone. It was better for me, really, because she had him to yell at instead. She was too busy to remember to go after me.

She didn't use her little girl voice much when Uncle Sid was around. I was glad. Sometimes I thought that baby voice was scarier than her yelling one.

He yelled, "Goddamn it, Isadora! You're stalled on the fucking train tracks!"

Then came her hook again: "Shut the fuck up! How can I concentrate?"

I tried to concentrate, but the words *train tracks* kept playing in my head. *Train tracks. Train tracks.* Cars honked at us now.

"Goddamn it, start the fucking car!" said Uncle Sid.

"Shut the fuck up! I can't concentrate!" My mom hooked back.

But there was a dinging now, and the lights on the long red-and-white-striped barriers started flashing. Then the gates came down, and we were on the wrong side of them. I dropped my book to the floor.

"Goddamn it, press the pedal down! Hurry the fuck up!"

"Shut the fuck up! I can't concentrate!"

Ding, ding, ding, ding! Ding, ding, ding, ding!

The red lights flashed back and forth, back and forth.

I heard someone crying. It was me.

The train was coming. I saw the white lights heading for us down the tracks.

I was screaming now. "Mom! Uncle Sid!"

But they didn't even hear me. They were just yelling and cursing. And the lights were flashing, and the bells were dinging, and we were gonna get hit. We were gonna get crushed!

There was a big horn blast! And the train was coming, it was coming, it was coming!

My hands pressed tight against my seat belt strap, squeezing, squeezing.

"Mom! Uncle Sid! Do something!"

I saw the train so close, those white lights were so close, and we were gonna get crushed.

Ding, ding, ding, ding! Ding, ding, ding, ding!

The car roared to life, and the stick made that dying duck sound, but it didn't stall—and we got through the space between the barriers, and the train passed right behind us. And I screamed and I screamed, and I was so, so scared. But they didn't even turn around. They just yelled and yelled and yelled, and we weren't going to Pancake Cottage—no way.

"Goddamn it! Let me drive!" said Uncle Sid.

"Shut the fuck up! I couldn't concentrate, that's all!"

In my head, the bells rang: *Ding, ding, ding, ding. Ding, ding, ding, ding.*

Six years later, sometimes they still did.

I woke to the serenade of two bows gliding across strings in a catchy harmony: a journey of two tones, similar yet different, one high, one low. Two opinionated rhythms, not clashing, but joining, intertwining.

I lay on the couch, listening, until Aunt Agatha and Axel finished playing. Chairs grated, pushed back against the metal floor. Axel and Aunt Agatha were talking, but I couldn't hear the words. Aunt Agatha said a bunch of stuff, and then Axel said his typical couple of words.

They went like that for a couple of rounds before I dragged myself off the couch and across the room.

"Morning," I said to them.

"Dear heart, this boy is a wonder," Aunt Agatha said. "A marvel. Help me convince him that he needs to go to Juilliard."

Wow, Juilliard. That was like the greatest music school in the world. If Aunt Agatha thought he should go there, she had to think he was good.

"You don't want to go to Juilliard?" I asked him.

"I can't commit to anything past getting up tomorrow morning, and even that's iffy."

Aunt Agatha shook her finger at Axel. "You're wasting your talent, young man."

I raised my eyebrows at Axel, telling him silently, "I told you so."

"If it's money you're worried about, I'm sure you can get a scholarship," said Aunt Agatha.

"It's not money," Axel said.

"Then what is it, darling?"

"I . . . I just can't jump into anything."

"That's no way to live, dear heart. You must pursue your passion. He who hesitates is lost! "

Axel sat back down and stared at his cello case, fingering the handle. He said in a low voice, "Agatha, I appreciate your suggestion, but right now, Juilliard's not for me."

Aunt Agatha didn't say anything for a moment. She wasn't used to objections. She watched Axel, who was flicking the case handle back and forth.

"All right, my dear. I hope you'll keep it in mind."

Axel, still flicking, nodded.

"Okay," Aunt Agatha said, clapping her hands together. "Who wants to get me some coffee?"

❀

Aunt Agatha and Axel were sipping coffee and eating buttered rolls, and I was crunching a carrot when Craig sauntered in. He nodded at us.

"Good morning, dear heart. I'd like you to meet Axel."

"Yo," Craig said to Axel.

Axel stared a minute, then said "Yo" back.

Craig nodded an acceptance of the greeting. Then he said, "Yo, you related to Axel Rose?"

"Yo, here's a hint, dude," said Axel. "When people are related, they have the same last names, not first names."

"Huh," said Craig. He turned to me. "S'up, baby."

Axel raised his eyebrows at me. I just shrugged.

As usual, Craig wore a shirt that could have been

painted on him. It was still early morning, but his skin had a sweaty gleam already.

Axel studied him, but Craig was oblivious. He nodded at us, then went to work.

Aunt Agatha stood. "Well, I'd better get started, too. You two relax. I know it's time-consuming to eat a carrot," she said. She ruffled my hair as she walked by.

Axel took a long sip of coffee and stared at Craig, who hammered away at a mahogany strip he'd positioned against the wall.

"That's the guy you work with every day?" Axel asked.

"Obviously."

"How old is he?"

"Twenty."

"He seems pretty . . . familiar with you."

"That's the way he is."

"Let's go outside," Axel said.

On the deck, Axel paced again. Back and forth. I watched, not really getting his problem.

Finally he stopped. "Willow . . . I . . . I'm worried about you."

"What are you talking about?"

"How you acted . . . what you said to me . . . "

"Hey, you said you were gonna forget that."

"I'm trying. It's just that when I saw this guy. . . . I feel like I need to protect you. It's like you're my little sister."

Great. That's just what I wanted to be. His freakin' kid sister.

"I told you, I don't need your protection."

"You are *fif*-teen, god-damn it." He pronounced each syllable slowly, through gritted teeth.

"Oh, but it was okay when you offered me vodka, wasn't it?"

He took a deep breath. "You're right. I never claimed to be the most responsible person ever, but I'm telling you you're making a mistake rushing into sex. Especially with a no-brainer like that guy!"

"It's none of your business, Axel."

"Maybe it's not, Willow." He stood there, frozen, looking like he was going to cry. "I'm sorry I even care. Believe me, I *am* sorry."

❀

Axel left, hoisting his cello down the ladder. I got dressed and went to work.

It was truly maddening, scraping gunk for hours on end. The only thing that helped was my iPod. Jim boomed in my ear, singing about the future being uncertain and the end always being near.

You said it, Jim.

I was busy concentrating when my headphones were suddenly lifted. Craig blinked in my face.

"What?" I asked, annoyed.

"Your aunt said she'll be back in an hour."

Wow, a complete, coherent sentence. Was this one of the seven signs?

"All righty. Can I have my headphones back?"

Oh boy, he was giving me that sexy look. *Houston, we have a problem.*

"S'up wit you an that guy?" *Oy, back butchering the English language.*

"We're friends."

"Friends?" He repeated the word like it was foreign. "Whatayamean?"

"You want me to explain the concept of friendship?"

"He doin' ya?" *This guy's gift with words just kept on giving.*

"No."

He scrunched his eyebrows together, puzzled. "Why not?"

"Because we're friends."

"That don't make no sense." *And he should know about not making sense.*

"He queer or somethin'?"

"Nooo."

Hmmm . . . was Axel gay or something?

He leaned in on me like Dracula coming in for the kill. But it wasn't my blood he was after.

"If ya don't got nothin' goin' on wit that guy, how 'bout we get somethin' goin'?"

I could smell the wild oats on his breath.

His hands were where they shouldn't have been— again. They were doing amazing things they shouldn't have been doing, either.

I was getting all tingly.

His lips crushed into mine. God help me, I actually

wanted to do it with him, even though he probably didn't remember my name.

I knew that tongue was coming; I prepared myself for it.

It slipped in. Swirled around. Found mine. They touched, tickled, tangled.

His hands were all the way up under my T-shirt. He unhooked my bra with one motion. I couldn't even do that myself. He groped my breasts, grabbed them roughly, then smoothly slid his palms across them.

He was guiding me toward the couch. . . .

He pushed me down, still kissing me. My head sank into the soft pillow, his lips attached to mine.

His body pressed on mine, pushing me hard against the lumpy cushions. Heavy, hot.

He pulled my T-shirt up, sucked on my breasts. My body felt like someone had set it on fire.

I had to end this. Now. Before he headed south.

"Craig . . . "

He continued. . . .

"Craig . . . stop."

He either didn't hear me or chose to ignore me.

I wacked him on the head. "Yo!" he said, popping up. "Whatsamatta now?"

"We . . . we don't have enough time."

"Who says?"

I propped myself up with my elbows. "Look, I'm too nervous about my aunt coming back."

He pushed me back down. "Ya been teasin' me a long time."

How had I been teasing him? By existing?

"When we gonna finish this?"

"Let me get back to you."

"How 'bout tanite?"

"No. Axel always comes over."

"Sunday." He whispered the word in my ear, then nibbled. "Your aunt works Sunday, right?"

"Yeah . . . but Axel . . . " he stopped my words with a deep kiss. Then he sucked on my neck, giving me goosebumps. The hell with it.

"All right, I'll get rid of Axel somehow. Sunday it is."

Ups and Downs 14

"Darlings, how's everything progressing?" Aunt Agatha pranced into the room.

My heart was still palpitating from my close encounter with Craig—and anticipating the even closer one planned for Sunday.

"Busy, busy," I said, plastering on what I hoped was an innocent smile to cover up all my dirty thoughts.

"Yo, Aggie," Craig said, waving his hammer. *Yo* was his all-purpose response. His statement in life. He was a yo-yo.

Good lord, I'd made a date to have sex with a yo-yo. *Was I insane?*

Then he shot me a look that struck the bull's-eye.

He was a yo-yo with some nifty tricks.

He resumed hammering. Aunt Agatha said in a low, serious voice, "Dear heart, you'll never believe what just happened to me."

I could say the same thing to her.

"I was getting out of my car, and one of the other boat owners approached me. He owns a large schooner, I believe. A huge, burly man. Quite intimidating. At any rate, he slung his arm around my shoulder, welcomed me, and said he was sorry he hadn't been to speak with me sooner. Then he proceeded to instruct me on how to hide drug cargo from the police."

She thought for a moment. "I think he called them 'the Feds,' actually."

"What made him think you wanted to know that?"

"I can't imagine. I guess it's simply because I'm here, with a large vessel. So I must be in the drug trade. I suppose the prospect of a virtuous project is inconceivable to some people."

I started to ask how you actually did hide drugs from the Feds, but decided I'd rather not know.

"What did you say to him?"

"The same thing I say to everyone. I thanked him profusely, said I'd remember his help, and gave him a little bow."

The thought of Aunt Agatha bowing to the drug trafficker cracked me up.

"Listen, dear heart, I know you've got that paint removal down to a science, but I wonder if you'd like to try something new?"

I almost jumped for joy. "Sure."

We went out to the back deck. She handed me a pair of work gloves and a brush. Then she bent to pry open a can of white paint with a screwdriver.

"So let me guess. We have to paint the whole outside of the barge," I said, pulling the gloves on.

"You got it, kiddo."

I wasn't even going to comment on the hugeness of the task. I needed to focus on a more pressing problem.

"Listen, I can't do the sides. That ledge is too narrow. I'll freak out and fall in. I'll help you with the front and back."

The truth is, I flip out in steep, tight places. I completely panic.

"We'll talk about that later."

God, why couldn't she just say okay?

"And then there's the roof, too."

The roof! "I don't think so, Aunt Agatha."

"Dear heart, you need to face your fears and conquer them. You'll be stronger for it."

Or I'll fall off the roof and die.

This was what I meant about arguing with the woman. She simply didn't allow it.

I sighed. "Let's just get started with this."

I dipped the fat brush into the bucket. "Hey, what about a roller?"

"Nah. That's the easy way out."

September couldn't come too soon.

I hit the disgusting green steel with the brush. Splat! White paint met the wall with a plop. My brush went up, down, up, down. Thick, fresh color spread satisfactorily.

"Amazing thing, paint," said Aunt Agatha, dipping her brush in.

I had to admit, this was fun. For now.

"Aw, smile, kid," Aunt Agatha said, nudging me with her elbow. "It won't kill you."

You never know. . . .

111

Aunt Agatha and I painted side by side in silence for a while. It was pretty darn hot, and I felt my face turning red. I was going to need some sunscreen if this was my new job.

"Willow?"

Hmmm . . . It was always trouble when she called me by my name. "Yeah?"

"Anything you want to talk about?"

Jesus, does she know about me and Craig?

"No."

"Sure?"

"Yup."

She took in a breath. "Axel mentioned something about a nightmare."

Traitor! "He did, huh?"

"He said you were in an emotional meltdown—those are his words."

Great, great. "Well, I think he exaggerated."

"Willow, why don't you talk to me about these things that are troubling you?"

Because you don't listen.

"Nothing's troubling me."

"I thought we were close."

How close can you be with someone who would have fit in perfectly in ancient Greece?

"We are."

"You can talk to me."

Sure, but will you hear what I'm saying?

"Everything's fine." I splattered paint against the wall angrily.

"Is it your mother?"

My mother. My father. Steve. You. The whole goddamn universe.

"Nothing's wrong."

"I can help you."

A seagull swooped in close, perhaps checking to see if anything on the deck was edible. He seemed to flash me the evil eye when he flapped away, empty-beaked.

I socked the wall with a huge splash. Jagged waves of paint jutted across the surface. The excess fell in drips down, down, down. I studied my creation like it was one of those ink splotch tests. What did it look like? *Let's see, a huge, ragged blob. It was me.*

"Nah, it's just a case of ego sickness. It'll pass."

"Oh, I see. You're using my words against me. Well, Willow, when I put my problems out of my mind—when I banish them as the illnesses they are, I'm healed. I stay humble. I know it's my ego that's making me worry."

"But just because something works for you doesn't mean it'll work for me."

She looked puzzled at the thought. "Are you saying your ego is above everyone else's?"

Oh my God. "No."

My ego is fucking dragging on the ground behind me. "Just forget it."

"Tell me about the dream."

"Why?"

"I want to help you overcome it."

Good luck. I sucked in a deep breath and let it out. "Fine. You want to know, I'll tell you."

I dropped the brush onto the deck and faced her.

113

"I wake up trapped in a black box. I can't see anything. It's just pitch black. I run into a wall. I turn, run into another wall. Four walls. I scream and scream, I pound and pound, but no one comes to help me. I finally collapse on the floor and curl up to wait to die."

I gave her a big-ass smile. "Happy?"

I waited for her to tell me it was my ego sending me the dream. I swear to God, I think I would have knocked her overboard.

"I know why you have that dream," she said quietly.

"Because of ego sickness?"

"No, dear heart. It really happened to you."

"I was trapped in a black box?"

"It was a small moving van. The back storage area."

"Wow."

The afternoon sun was beaming in my eye. I looked down at the deck, speckled white from our paint drops.

"I thought it was a metaphor for the hopelessness of my life."

"Don't be so dramatic, darling."

"So what happened to me?"

"You fell asleep in the van while your mother and I were moving things into the house you live in now. I had to run a few errands. She finished going in and out, and wanted to start organizing inside. She didn't want to wake you, so she locked you in to make sure you'd be safe."

"And she didn't think I'd wake up."

"Apparently not. You know your mother. She doesn't always think things through before acting. As I said, she was trying to make sure you were safe."

"Please. She probably didn't want me to wake up because I'd ask for something, like food, and she'd have to stop what she was doing to take care of me."

"I doubt that was her motive. . . ."

"Yeah, well, doubt on. I don't."

Aunt Agatha sighed. Suddenly, she looked old and weary.

"Yeah, so I guess Mom didn't bother to check on me? See if I woke up? Or maybe if I was suffocating back there or something?"

"I don't know how long it was until you woke up. It could have been minutes or . . . longer. I was gone about an hour and a half. When I pulled up, I asked your mother where you were. She told me. You know she has no concept of time."

Was that supposed to be an excuse?

Aunt Agatha continued, "She didn't remember the last time she'd checked on you."

Nor did she care, probably.

"I unlocked the van. You were curled in a fetal position against the back wall, shaking and rocking."

I stared at the bobbing boats surrounding us, felt the barge moving up and down ever so slightly. I tried to decide if this was better or worse than my mind having created the whole ordeal. It was a draw.

"So now that you know what's behind the dream, you can drop it."

Oh, sure. I could just drop it. Cut it out like a useless appendage.

Everything was so simple for Aunt Agatha. Set your

mind on autopilot toward freedom from your problems and demons.

I didn't feel liberated. I just felt numb.

If only it could be like Aunt Agatha said. But for me, everything was a burden. Life was a burden, and I was the mule carting it around. And the path was dark. Very, very dark.

Intoxicated

"Hey, Benedict," I said to Axel when he walked in.

"Excuse me?"

"You're a damn jackass, you know that?"

"I've suspected it. Thanks for the confirmation."

"Don't get all sarcastic." *That was my role, thank you very much.* "You had a lot of nerve telling my aunt about my dream."

"I was just trying to help you."

"Yeah, well, how 'bout I call your dad, to try and help you?"

He looked down. "Point taken."

"What, now you're gonna get all sad again? I've got one word for you, Axel, and that word is Prozac."

Man, I was leaning into him. I was pissed.

"I'm gonna go now," he said to the floor.

Oh, jeez. "Come on, lighten up. Here's an idea. Why don't you go back to your boat and get us some vodka?"

He looked at me with those pathetically sad eyes. I really felt like smacking him or shaking him or something. I mean, I was sad, too. But I, like, functioned. Most of the time, anyway. It's the humor that got me through. Even though it was mostly at my own expense. Hey, if you couldn't pick on yourself, who could you pick on?

I was really in the mood to try some vodka. "Seriously, dude, go get it."

He just stood there, shoulders all slouched. A real downer, just when I was trying to pull myself out of the gutter. I was almost positive that vodka would give me a boost up. Sure, Aunt Agatha could just will herself to let go of things, but some of us mere mortals needed a little help.

"Earth to Axel," I said, waving my hand in front of his face.

"If that's what you want. . . ."

"It is."

I was going to break out of this goddamn fog of doom. And then, for toppers, I was going to have sex on Sunday. *Yee-ha*.

Axel left and then schlepped back with the citrus vodka, a nice full bottle. I grabbed it from his hands.

"You bring glasses?" I asked.

He shook his head no.

Loser, I thought. He hung his head again, like I'd said the thought out loud.

I felt like conking him on the head with the vodka. "Cheer up, will ya? We can take slugs straight from the bottle." I twisted the cap open. "Unless sharing germs offends you. Might be too close to kissing, and I know you don't want to do that."

Boy, I was in rare form. I really didn't expect to say that. It just came out.

"You know, Willow, I think I should go."

"You gonna make me drink alone?" I raised the bottle, tilted it against my lips.

His hand shot up, pushed the angle of the bottle down a little. "Hey, be careful. That stuff's potent."

I snorted at the thought of being careful. Unfortunately, I chose that same moment to chug down a mouthful of vodka. I gagged and spit. Axel wound up wearing my shot on his T-shirt.

He raised his eyebrows, and then he laughed.

I laughed, too.

"I guess I'm gonna have to show you how to hold your alcohol," he said. "Just take a little sip."

I tried it again. A little, like he said. It didn't really taste like anything, except lemons, but it burned the heck out of my throat. I coughed and passed him the bottle.

"So, people like this stuff?"

"It beats gin," he said, taking a gulp.

We went on the front deck and settled down with our backs against the wall. He was still looking pretty stiff.

I took another sip of the vodka. It still burned. I waited for the euphoria.

"So, when does this stuff kick in?"

"Soon," he said. "Real soon, for you."

We passed the bottle back and forth a few more times,

119

me taking nips, him basically guzzling. His body loosened up, his shoulders relaxed; he stretched his legs out and crossed them at the ankles.

"How do you feel now?" he asked me.

"I feel good!" I said. Actually, I sang it. Then I sang more: "I knew that I would, now."

There are things that I would not normally do, and on top of that list is bursting into song in front of someone. But at that moment, music was in my heart and it just had to come out.

"I feel nice. Like sugar and spice."

"That was excellent. You should go join a band or something," said Axel.

"Really?"

"Nooo."

We both laughed again. I giggled so hard I ached all over.

"So I guess the stuff's kicking in?" I asked. Axel was looking a little fuzzy.

"Oh, yeah. It kicked you real good."

We had a blast. I never laughed so much in my life, even though I wasn't sure what was so funny. We sat there and bullshitted, and the sky went from day to night, and we just laughed and laughed. *Why hadn't I tried alcohol sooner?*

"So you like the vodka?" Axel asked.

I hiccuped. "What's not to like?"

Suddenly, I felt dizzy and nauseated. Bile rose up my throat. Before I could even think to get up, I puked all over my lap.

"Well, there's that," Axel said.

❋

If that night had been the most amusing, the next morning was the most horrific. They must call it getting hammered because the day after, you sure feel like somebody whacked you with one.

I'd dreamed I had a throbbing headache, and when I opened my eyes, I found out it was real. Blinking caused major pain. And I felt unbelievably queasy.

My hair swung in my face, and I nearly puked again from the scent of barf in it. I sniffed my skin, and my stomach lurched. My whole body smelled of puke. So did my clothes. *That's what I got for using myself as a bucket.*

I attempted to sit up. Pain shot through my brain, and the room spun. Now I knew why I'd waited so long to try alcohol. I couldn't even remember going to bed. After I'd puked, everything went blank.

"Hey, you're awake." Axel's voice came from behind me. "I brought you something." He gave me a roll.

"I can't eat this. I'm on a diet," I told him, handing it back.

He pushed it on me again. "Listen, Willow. You sure as hell don't need a diet, but even if you did, today's not the day to count carbs. You need to get something solid into your system, or you'll be sick all day. You drank on an empty stomach last night, didn't you?"

I nodded. "Except for the carrots."

"Yeah, I know. I could tell by what came up. Orange bile. Why didn't you eat yesterday?"

I shrugged. I didn't know why I did or didn't do anything anymore.

"Well, eat the roll."

I picked off a piece of the crust and stuck it in my mouth.

He leaned closer and said, "I didn't tell your aunt about the drinking, obviously, but I had to tell her you got sick. I mean, you reek. I cleaned you up as best I could, but you need a shower."

"Well, guess what. I'm not getting it here. We don't have one."

He raised his eyebrows at that. "Okay, come over and take one on my boat."

I got up, and the room twirled. I leaned onto Axel, closed my eyes, and hoped it would pass. It finally ended enough that I could walk, slowly.

I felt like complete shit.

"Eat some more bread," he said.

"Must I?"

"Unless you wanna try the one sure way to beat a hangover."

"Yeah? What?"

"Get drunk again."

The thought of vodka twisted my stomach. "I'll pass," I said, biting off a hunk of roll.

"Dear heart," Aunt Agatha said as I lurched toward her with clean clothes in my hands. "How do you feel?"

I sure wasn't going to burst into song. "Lousy."

"I'm so sorry to hear you were ill last night. Must be some sort of virus."

"Absolutely," I said.

Behind me, Axel snickered.

I told her I was going to take a shower. Then I headed out the door, with Axel following.

I walked straight into Craig.

"Yo, baby." He didn't see Axel behind the door, and he reached his hand out, most likely to touch me obscenely somewhere. I slapped it down.

"What the . . . oh, hey, man," Craig said. Apparently, spotting Axel had shocked the "yo" out of him.

"Yo," said Axel with a curt nod.

He just wasn't liking Craig. I couldn't imagine why.

I moved back, partly because Axel was there and partly because I didn't want Craig to get a whiff of barf. Not that it would matter to him, most likely. Animal instinct would prevail, especially in someone who hadn't progressed much past the Neanderthal stage.

"Where ya 'goin'?"

"I'm taking a shower at Axel's."

Craig's eyes narrowed. He looked from me to Axel to me again. Clearly, to him it wasn't possible I'd take the shower solo.

He needed to go scrub his filthy mind.

"See ya Sunday?"

Oy. Big-mouthed schmuck. "Yeah, yeah. Sunday. Meet me at the front gate at noon." I threw in the front gate thing to throw Axel off.

Of course, I threw Craig off. He looked confused, but nodded.

❁

We were walking along the dock when Axel finally blew his cork. "So?"

"So what?"

"So what the hell are you doing with that scumbag on Sunday at noon?"

"I promised I'd tutor his sister in English. She's flunking in summer school, poor thing." I can lie real smoothly, if I have a few minutes' advance notice.

Axel looked suspicious. "Willow . . ."

"Can we hurry up? The smell of me is making me sick."

He didn't quite believe me, but he couldn't provide evidence beyond a reasonable doubt.

"Okay, okay."

I felt much better after I was washed clean of the barf. I still felt a throbbing in my head, but it was more like a small hammer hitting me now, instead of a mallet.

I squeezed into my clothes in the tiny bathroom. I think they call boat bathrooms *heads* because you can't fit more than your head in comfortably.

I gingerly wrapped my hair in a towel, managing to knock all Axel's crap off the sink with the towel when I flipped it around my hair. Then I banged my head against the sink while picking up the hairbrush, nail clipper, toothpaste, toothbrush, disposable razors, shaving cream, and deodorant.

Jesus, did he put anything away? I checked the storage compartment under the sink. *No, he did not.*

Grabbing the hairbrush, I stepped into the main cabin.

Axel was reading *Much Ado About Nothing*. *Hey, at least it was a comedy.* That boy needed to lighten up.

"Good play? I never read that one," I said.

He nodded, still reading.

"What's your favorite line in it?" I was sure he had one.

"I am gone, though I am here," he rattled mechanically.

Unbelievable. He managed to find doom and gloom in everything.

He looked up. "You got dressed in there? You could have used my cabin. I mean, it's not much bigger, but it's a little better."

"I didn't want to parade in front of you in a towel."

"All right, can we can the sarcasm? We need to get past that shit."

"I'm sorry." I really was. I didn't know why I got like that.

"It's okay."

I sat across from him and started brushing my hair. I bent and tossed my hair over gently, to unknot the underside.

After a few moments, he asked, "So what did your aunt say?"

"About?"

"About the dream."

"Pretty much what I thought—that I should wipe it from my head."

"Just like that?"

I flipped my hair back up and faced Axel. "Well, there was one bit of interesting news. It turns out the dream was real. I was locked in the back of a moving van when I was little."

"Gee, Willow. Sorry to hear that." He got up and hugged me. "You think you're gonna be able to get past it now?"

The tears welled up again. *This was getting ridiculous. I could open my own sprinkler company.*

I rubbed my eyes across his T-shirt and sniffed.

"There's so much to get past, Axel. . . . I don't know where to begin."

Sound and Fury

The next night, I lay on the couch, too nervous to sleep. Tomorrow was d-day. D for de-virginizing.

I was past worrying if Craig was the right guy. He wasn't. But he sure made me feel good. That had to count for something. I didn't mean anything to him. But he didn't mean anything to me, either. I was using him. Kind of.

We all want the first time to be so special, like Cinderella being swept up by Prince Charming. But I doubt that their relationship was perfect, anyway. *I bet they wound up divorced.*

Is anybody happy, really?

I had to take what I could get, and what I could get right now was a smoking hot guy who regarded me as some kind of plaything. But at least he regarded me. And he was sooo good at strumming my strings.

In the morning, Aunt Agatha leaned over the top of the couch and smiled at me. "Feeling better, dear heart?"

"Headache's gone." *Heartache's not.*

"Good, good. You slept late. It's eleven o'clock."

Eleven o'clock! I had to meet Craig in an hour. I jumped up.

"You missed Axel this morning. He played duets with me again."

"That's nice." I was rummaging around for my clothes.

"He's a wonderful boy. Intelligent, witty, thoughtful . . . "

"Yes, yes he is." *But no time to chat about him now. I had a date with his polar opposite.*

I pawed through the pile of clothes in my bag. *Dang. Where were my clean blue shorts? I needed to do laundry.*

"I just don't understand his lack of motivation. What does he do on that boat all day?"

"Reads and plays his cello." *Whew.* I found the shorts near the bottom of the suitcase. I must have passed over them three times.

"Indeed. Well, I suppose there's worse things an eighteen-year-old might do. Still, I wish we could convince him to attend Juilliard. He's wasting his talent."

"Yeah, we can't have talent being wasted, that's for sure," I said, grabbing my bra, underwear, and purple T-shirt.

It was kind of funny, she seemed more interested in Axel's future than mine. Guess I should have pursued that violin.

"Well, I have to run to work." She gave me a peck on the cheek. "Have a good day, darling."

If she only knew how good a day it was going to be.

The noon sun was brutal, boy, especially after stepping out of a cave. What they needed around the boatyard was some nice tall, leafy trees for shade. To get any now, you'd have to crawl under one of those disabled boats in dry dock.

The sweat started beading when I hit the ladder. *Attractive*.

Craig was waiting at the gate for me, leaning on the fence with one leg propped up. On him, sweat looked damn good.

He gave me a wink. "Where we goin'?"

"Well, I was hoping you had someplace to go." *You being twenty and all*.

"Can't go ta my crib. Mom's back from church."

Fabulous. "How about a motel or something?"

"Got no cash. Aggie paid me on Friday. Spent it already."

Oy. "So I guess you want to go to the barge?"

He shrugged. *Big on ideas, this guy*.

"I really didn't want to do that. Axel lives across the dock. If he sees us . . . "

"We'll sneak there."

"Yeah. It's real easy to sneak up a ladder in broad daylight." *He really was a schmuck*.

He grabbed my arm, pulled me against him, ran his hand up my back to the base of my neck, electrifying me.

"Okay, we'll sneak there," I said.

❈

We crunched across the gravel, then walked through the maze of boats to get to the back dock entrance. That way, we wouldn't go near Axel's boat.

I was nervous now. The threat of getting caught made me realize the insanity of this little adventure.

For all Craig's raw sex appeal, that wasn't the reason I was doing this; not really. I was doing it so I could be like everyone else—to be accepted. Be normal.

I wouldn't be the bookworm anymore. I would be one of *them*. I could get involved in a conversation about sex instead of overhearing bits and pieces and not understanding what they were talking about. I just wanted to have something in common with the rest of the world.

Being alone sucked. If I wiped the scarlet "V" off my chest, maybe things would be different in September. It was my only hope.

Above my head, a flock of seagulls cawed wildly, wickedly, loudly.

Maybe this was insane, but I was doing it to keep from going mad.

Axel wasn't on his deck, thank God.

Craig followed me up the ladder and inside the barge. He was on me before I even got the door closed. His hands moved so fast, they felt like they were everywhere at once. His mouth was on mine, his tongue inside. It was like he was fast-forwarding to the part where we'd stopped. Then he skipped ahead.

My heart felt like it was heading on a crash course right through my chest.

His kiss was aggressive, and I couldn't breathe.

I pushed him off of me.

"What? What?" He was annoyed.

"You need to slow down. I can't even catch my breath."

He stared at me. "Yo, I know what your problem is. You're a virgin."

I nodded, still trying to bring my heart rate down from four digits.

His lips widened into a huge smile. "I thought so, first time we got cozy." He came close, brushed his hand against my cheek, sending a rush through me.

"'Kay. I'll go slow. I never been wit a virgin before."

He took me in his arms. His hands went under my shirt, then performed his amazing bra unfastening act again.

He glided me around all the wood and crap toward the couch, all the while sending hot chills through me and kissing me softly.

My butt brushed against a sawhorse with a box of nails on it, sending 500 metal spikes pinging across the floor, yet we moved on through the debris unscathed.

I glanced at the incomplete mahogany wall—the half constructed puzzle. Would all the pieces ever fit completely? Would mine?

I closed my eyes and let Craig take me over. It wasn't hard to do. His fingertips glided around and around, arousing sensations and raising me up like a jet, rising higher and higher.

He lifted me onto the couch, my eyes still closed. My head nestled on my pillow like it was a cloud. I was floating, floating. . . .

Then I felt him tug at my shorts as he began pulling them down.

"Hey, I thought we were taking this slow."

"Chill, girl."

That knocked me from the sky. It sounded a little too much like a canine command. *Stay, girl.*

He continued, "I'm not doin' *that* yet. I'm doin' something else. Ya'll like it."

He climbed back up and gave me a deep kiss meant to placate me, like he was throwing a dog a treat. *Good doggie.*

"Just tell me one thing," I yipped.

He hovered over me. "Yeah?"

"What's my name?"

His face fogged. His eyebrows scrunched together. This was a tough one.

"Uhhh . . .Willa?" His eyes were lusty; his smell was musky. The devil was in his touch. *God help me.*

"Close enough," I said, but I was trembling.

"Hey, relax," he said. "I'm not gonna hurtcha, for Christ's sake. No one's ever done this to ya?"

I shook my head no.

"SweartaGod, strike me dead, you're gonna like this."

The good news was that God wasn't going to be hurling any lightning bolts. But I sure felt like I'd been struck with one.

Craig may not have been a master of language, but he could put his mouth to good use. Speaking was overrated, anyway. I should know, having lost my power of speech for a few minutes myself.

"Your turn."

I looked at him blankly, my mind still in orbit over my body.

"Ya do me now."

Uck.

I didn't want to do *that*.

It sounded so gross.

"I don't think I can. . . ."

"'Course you can. Just don't bite."

I didn't have the slightest desire to bite.

I tried to do what he wanted.

He moaned. He wouldn't let go of my head, allowing me only the slightest movement. I was choking, gagging. I thought I might throw up. I sputtered, hacking desperately.

He finally released me. I fell back into my pillow, coughing, wheezing, gulping deep breaths with incredible appreciation for the air I could finally take in.

"Ready?"

Oh my God, now he wanted to have sex? What the hell was that going to be like?

No, I thought. *No, no.*

"No," I said.

He stared at me for a second, blinking like he didn't get it. "What?"

"No, I can't do it." I hoisted myself, tried to get up. But he was leaning over me, and he wasn't budging.

"What da hell ya mean?" His voice was ugly. He grabbed my wrist and squeezed. "Listen, bitch. I gave ya something. Now it's payback time."

"But . . . but I just . . ." *I almost died.*

"Ya gotta finish me off now."

"No," I said.

I kicked at him.

He slapped his palm across my face. It stung—and stunned me. Nobody'd ever hit me before.

He yanked at my hair. "Just lie still, and let's finish this nicely."

Nicely? Oh my God. . . . I tried to hit him, but he got me first—again.

He leaned down full force on me. "I said, lie still."

Craig had turned into a monster. He was blurry from all my tears pouring down. He looked like some kind of specter out of a nightmare: something that's hunting you, but you can't quite make it out. The boogeyman.

I was crying and saying, "No."

He slapped me again. "Shut the fuck up!"

I realized he was going to force himself in.

I tried to kick him, but I couldn't move. He was just too strong for me. He'd pinned my arms under my own body, which was pinned under him.

I reached my head up and bit him on the arm.

"Fuckin' bitch!" He put his hand over my neck and squeezed. I thought he was going to kill me.

I gulped, trying to calm down. But I could still breathe;

I could swallow. The pressure on my neck hurt, but he didn't mean to kill me. At least not yet.

Then a voice came from across the room: "Holy shit!" I couldn't see who it was, but I recognized that voice immediately—Axel.

All he could see was Craig's head over the couch. Craig clamped one hand over my mouth and continued to squeeze my throat with the other. I couldn't get out a sound.

He peered over the couch at Axel. "Yo, ya mind, man? Kinda busy here."

I fought like crazy to get his hand off my mouth, but I just couldn't. He pressed into my neck even tighter.

Axel had to know it was me under Craig. He knew I was meeting him.

"I hear ya. Just came to pick up the sheet music I left here."

His voice was soft. I could just bet that he was staring at the floor.

I had to get his attention, let him know I didn't want this. Craig's legs had shifted slightly and I could move my knee. I only had one shot. If I missed . . .

I rammed my knee into Craig. He screamed and let go of my mouth and throat.

"Axel! Axel!" I rasped, coughing.

I kneed Craig again and shoved him off me enough so that I could pull myself out from under him. I rolled onto the floor, pulled my shorts up, and ran.

"Axel! Oh my God . . ." I threw myself into his arms, making him drop his music. Sheets scattered all over the floor.

"What the fuck's up?"

"I . . . I gotta go outside. . . . I can't breathe in here." I clung to him, shaking. We walked slowly. I wouldn't let him go.

Outside, I blinked in the harsh sunlight, but I was so grateful to see it.

"What happened? I don't understand."

"He . . . he had his hands over my mouth . . . and . . . had me by the throat. I . . . I was trying to scream."

"What?"

"He . . . wouldn't let me go. He had me pinned under him. . . ." I was coughing from the throbbing pain, plus all the tears clogging my throat.

"He *hurt* you?" Axel's face turned dark red. His eyes were fiery.

Craig chose that moment to burst through the doorway. It probably wasn't his best timing.

"You son of a *bitch*!" Axel lowered me to the deck and moved into Craig's face.

"Yo, man, I dunno what she's sayin', but she axed for it."

Axel backed Craig against the wall. He leaned right into Craig, grabbed up the neck of his T-shirt. "Even if she did, she's *fifteen*!"

"So?"

"*So?* That's called statutory rape, you stupid motherfucker!"

"Getouttahere."

"He . . . hit me," I said. "He hit me . . . and . . . choked me and . . . held me down. . . . "

136

Axel put his hand around Craig's throat and banged his head against the steel wall of the barge.

"You like doing that to a helpless girl? Make you feel tough? Like a man?"

"Yo, sw-sweartaGod, sh-she wanted it." Craig's voice sounded all pinched. And shaky. Then Craig told him what I'd done . . . what he'd made me do. . . .

Axel's hand dropped.

Craig pushed past him and headed toward the edge of the deck to get away from him.

I was hysterical. "I did . . . do that . . . but he forced me—my—" *God, I couldn't say it.* "He forced my head down . . . held it down. I was gagging. . . . I couldn't breathe!" I buried my face in my hands, squeezing my eyes shut to make it all go away.

I felt arms around me. "It's okay, Willow," Axel said.

I kept my eyes clamped shut. "Then he . . . he said . . . I owed him more. He said I had to . . . to finish him off. . . . "

"Yo, man. I didn't even get ta do it! Ya walked in on us!"

"So maybe I should hand her over to you right now?" Axel snarled.

I opened my eyes. Craig looked like he was considering Axel's offer.

"You *goddamn bastard*!" Axel exploded. He jumped up and charged at Craig.

"She fuckin' wanted it!" Craig insisted, teetering at the edge of the deck.

"No, Craig!" I screamed through my aching throat. "I said *no*!"

"Ya said no when it was too late!" Craig yelled at me.

"It's never too late, you fucking *prick*," Axel said. "Maybe you'll learn to respect the word *no* in jail, when *you* try using it."

"Whatayamean, jail?"

"For sexual assault."

"Assault?"

"You don't know what *assault* means?" Axel smashed his fist into Craig's face, tossing him overboard. There was a huge splash. "*That's* what *assault* means, you asshole." He spat into the water.

I sat curled up with my arms around my knees, rocking a little, trying to stop the shaking.

Craig was making gurgling noises and spewing curses from the water.

Axel came back over to me. He put one arm around me and took out his cell phone with the other.

"Who're you calling?"

"The cops."

"No. . . . It was my fault."

"It was *not* your fault. I want you to remember that. *That's* why I'm calling."

"But I agreed to meet him. . . ."

Behind us, there was still splashing and cursing as Craig swam to the dock to haul himself up.

"I'm sure he was very persuasive." He looked into my eyes. "Look, I knew you were lying to me yesterday, but I figured, what could I really do? You had your mind made up. Then, when I saw him on that couch, knowing you were under him, part of me wanted to rip him the fuck off of you. But I knew I couldn't stop you from doing it some other time." He stopped. "But he tried to force you. . . . There's no way I'm gonna let him get away with that."

"What . . . what am I gonna tell my aunt?"

"I'll handle her. You don't have to worry about anything. I'll take care of you."

"Who's gonna do all the work he did?"

"I will." He kissed my forehead.

"Oh my God, I'm so sorry. . . . " I started crying again.

"It's *not* your fault." He squeezed me tight, flipping his phone open and dialing 911 with his free hand.

"Remember, Willow. It's not your fault."

Stand by Me

Everything was a big, blurred mess after that. Sirens and cops everywhere. It was like they called in the SWAT team.

They sure didn't need one. Craig wasn't hard to miss. He wasn't fleeing or hiding. He was just standing on the dock, dripping and still cursing at us like a madman when they got there.

They hauled his soggy ass off in cuffs.

Watching that made me feel worse. Guilty, like it was my fault he was under arrest. And scared. *Would he come back after he made bail?*

The cops wanted me to tell them what happened, but I just couldn't. All I could do was cry and cry and cry. I'd fucked everything up so badly.

Axel told them what I'd told him. They said they'd get my statement later. Jesus, how could I tell them? How could I tell anyone? Axel didn't even know everything. . . .

They said I had to go to the hospital. To get examined. To have pictures taken. I didn't want anyone to touch me.

And the last thing I wanted was to be photographed. But I had to go. Axel said I had to.

He promised to stay with me.

We were going in an ambulance, me on a stretcher like I *was* in an accident or something. I was the accident. A freak.

The paramedics tried to strap a blanket over me. I completely flipped. I could not be confined like that—there was just no way. They said I had to be strapped for safety, that I couldn't be transported without it.

Axel calmed me down and had them do the strap real loose. He showed me that I could unbuckle it myself.

Axel was so good to me. Too good to me.

He told them he was my brother. That way, they'd let him stay with me.

Axel had an argument with the driver, because he didn't want them to take me to the hospital a few blocks away. He said the building looked like it was going to cave in from the outside and he could only imagine the conditions on the inside.

Then he said they couldn't take me to any hospital in Queens or Brooklyn. He insisted they take me to a hospital in Manhattan. The driver said no way, because that was forty minutes away, at least. Axel told him that the elitist snob in him was rearing its ugly head and no one was taking his little sister anywhere but Manhattan.

Then he took out a hundred-dollar bill and gave it to the driver. He said the ambulance company could bill him for the transportation—the hundred was for the driver and the other paramedic.

They took me to midtown. NYU Medical Center. Axel held my hand the whole way.

All that time, the only thing running through my head was, *What would Axel think when he found out the whole truth?*

Axel filled out all the papers for me. Again, he claimed to be my brother.

They asked how they could contact our mother.

Axel took one look at me, then said that our mom was dead.

What about our father?

He was dead, too.

He put Aunt Agatha down as my guardian, but he explained that she couldn't be reached for a couple of hours. It was true, she was probably in the middle of driving or performing or something.

God, I couldn't face her.

But what about the insurance forms? What kind did we have? Who would be authorizing payment to the hospital?

Axel tossed his platinum American Express card on the counter.

Since my "brother" was eighteen, he was allowed to consent to my treatment.

I wouldn't get examined without Axel there holding my hand. I knew it was a lot to ask, but I was beyond scared.

The nurse said, "Don't worry; it's just like going to the gynecologist." But I'd never been to the gynecologist.

I burst into more tears, and Axel asked to please be allowed in. Finally, she agreed. Since he was my brother.

I went behind a screen and changed into the blue gown with the ties in the back that they gave me. When I came out, Axel stared at me in the stark white light that showed off all my bruises.

"That bastard nailed you good." He had. I'd looked in the full-length mirror. My mouth, cheek, neck, and arms were all blotched with purple. So were my thighs, although Axel couldn't see them.

Holding onto my gown, I climbed onto the examining table with the crinkly white paper pulled over it and the metal things sticking up on either side. It was slanted, so I wound up half sitting, half lying—which added to my total humiliation.

I reached for Axel's hand again. He was the only reason I could even stand doing this, the only reason I didn't just collapse onto the floor into a ball of shame.

Oh my God, oh my God.

"It's okay, Willow. I'll help you through this. Please stop crying," Axel said, wiping at my tears. *Talk about asking the impossible.*

A girl came in. She was probably in her twenties. She introduced herself as a rape crisis counselor. She said she was there to talk and that she'd stay and explain what the doctor was doing to me. I told her to go away.

She looked all right, nice and everything, not drippy or syrupy. But I didn't want to talk to anyone but Axel. She said I could call her anytime. I said I wouldn't. Axel took her card and thanked her.

The doctor finally came in, a sour-looking old man who unrolled his metal tools onto his little work table without so much as a hello.

He told me to put my legs on the metal things—he called them *stirrups*. There I was, spread open again. *God, why couldn't everyone just leave me alone?*

My gown slipped a little.

"Jesus, that fucking piece of shit," Axel said, staring at the exposed bruises on my thighs.

The doctor snapped on rubber gloves. Then he draped what looked and felt like a huge thick napkin with a plastic coating over my legs. He put a glob of petroleum jelly on his gloved finger and disappeared behind the napkin.

It hurt to have my legs spread like that. I mean, my whole body ached, anyway. I just thanked God I couldn't see what he was doing down there. It was so damned uncomfortable, though, with him poking around. And mortifying.

I kept squirming; the paper kept crinkling.

"Hold still, please," the doctor said in a flat-liner voice.

Then he pushed some metal thing into me, and I screamed. It hurt, and it was cold, and I was shaking.

I just wanted to crawl somewhere and die.

Axel squeezed my hand. "It's all right, Willow. He'll be done soon."

But it wasn't all right.

"Why, why are you doing this to me?" I yelled at the brute behind the napkin. "He didn't rape me."

The doctor wheeled his little stool around and looked directly at my face for the first time.

"We have to check for bruising no matter what, miss, and for DNA."

Oh, God. DNA. They were going to find out.

I cried even more when he grabbed the long cotton swab stick from his tray and then went back under the drape, stuck it in, and scraped around.

"C'mon, Willow. It's only cotton. It can't hurt that much. Please, calm down." Poor Axel looked so worried. But I wasn't crying because of the pain. It was the shame. They'd all know now.

Axel would know.

The doctor grabbed another stick. He swabbed my mouth and throat too, which made me think of Craig telling Axel about the blow job.

God, I just wanted to die. That was really, really all I asked.

I didn't even know how Axel could look at me, knowing I did that.

Then the doctor took a bunch of pictures—of my whole body. *Great*. Just the thing I wanted done at that moment in my life.

Axel turned his back to us when the doctor examined and photographed my breasts.

Finally, the doctor said I could get dressed. But before I could even drag my ass off the table, a nurse came in. She said two police officers were waiting to talk to me. They'd driven in all the way from Rockaway. And for about the billionth time, I cried.

Axel wrapped himself around me. "You're almost through this, sweetheart. I promise you. Be strong. I'll be here for you."

"But, but . . ."

"What is it?" he asked.

I tugged at the white paper sticking out from under me, ripped a piece off. "I . . . I can't say it."

"You can tell me anything."

Rip, rip. "No . . . you'll hate me. . . ."

"I could never hate you. And I told you, this is not your fault."

I closed my eyes and listened to the beat of my feet thumping against the table. "But it is. . . . It . . . is. I let him. . . . I let him. . . . "

"What?"

"Before everything . . . went wrong. . . ."

"Will you please just tell me?"

I sucked in a huge breath and let it out. Then I opened my eyes and tried to tell him. "Before the bl . . . before he got angry. . . he . . . I let him. . . . He went . . . down there. With his mouth."

"He went down on you."

I didn't know it was called that. I nodded.

"So?"

"I . . . I . . . I . . . ." I just couldn't say it.

"What?"

"I . . . I liked it. A lot."

"Okay . . ."

"Don't you see? It's my fault. I let everything get started. I let him do that . . . so then I owed him something." I leaned on Axel, sobbed into his shoulder. "And now . . . the DNA's gonna prove it was my fault."

He clutched me as I shook and cried. It seemed like there was no limit to my tears.

He said softly, "You don't have to feel guilty about liking it. It's normal. Okay?"

I nodded, but continued to cry.

"And no matter what he gave you, no matter how good he made you feel, he did not have the right to touch you—to take any so-called payback—once you said no. Do you understand, Willow?"

I didn't. I wished I did, but I didn't. I just felt wrong. Dirty.

He moved me back from his shoulder and scrutinized my face. "This is *not* your fault. God, why can't I make you see that?"

I shrugged, looked at the floor. It *was* my fault. To think that I'd been so desperate . . . that I'd allowed, if not started the chain of events that had led to this—

He handed me the toothbrush and mini-tube of toothpaste the nurse had given me with the gown. "Go brush your teeth. Get dressed. We'll talk about this later. Right now, you're gonna tell your story to the cops. And don't worry about what anyone's gonna think." He hugged me

147

again and whispered into my ear, "Just tell your story, and then we'll go home."

❈

Axel called a car service to bring us back to Far Rockaway. We could've gone back with the cops, but he didn't think the back of a patrol car was the best place for me right now.

I still couldn't stop trembling. We went into the gift shop while we were waiting for our ride. He bought me a big soft throw blanket with teddy bears on it. I felt kind of stupid with the teddy bears, but it was all they had and it was warm.

It was dark already and drizzling. We stood outside the hospital under an awning. City traffic rushed down the slick street, tires swishing in the wetness. Everyone was always in a hurry in Manhattan, even in the rain on a Sunday evening. It was like a rule or something.

A shiny black Lincoln town car, beaded with water drops, pulled up for us. I huddled against Axel in the back seat, shivering in spite of my blanket and aching, all the way through the Midtown Tunnel, across the Long Island Expressway, down Queens Boulevard, all the way back to Rockaway.

Everything was sore. My bruises, the insides of my mouth and throat, and my heart. I swear to God, I just wanted to fling open the car door and throw myself onto the road.

Axel held on tight to me. It was like he knew that I

might just go for it, if I had the chance. It was like he knew that I just wanted to be done.

Axel had to get out and unlock the chain on the boat-yard fence before the driver could pull into the gravel road. Axel asked him to pull up close to the dock. He wanted to minimize my walking. He signed the credit card slip, instructed the driver to close the gate behind him and padlock it again, and then we trudged off.

Suddenly, I was filled with panic. "What about Aunt Agatha? She didn't know where I was all this time!"

"I left her a note. I just said you were with me. That's all. I . . . I thought she should find out what happened in person."

"Axel . . . I can't face her. I really can't. And I can't lie on that couch, either. Please, can I sleep on your boat?"

"Uh . . . I guess so. I don't know what your aunt's gonna say."

"Don't make me go on the barge tonight."

"Okay, okay. I'll settle you in, then I'll go talk to your aunt."

I gripped his hand again. "Thanks."

We climbed aboard Axel's boat and went below. I followed him into his small cabin at the front of the hold. The walls curved into a point. Axel's cello case stood against the left wall. There was a door—probably to a closet—on the right wall. After a few feet of walking space, the rest of the cabin was all bed, reaching to the tip.

"You sleep in here. I'll go on one of the couches," Axel said.

I dropped my blanket, climbed under the sheets, and curled into a ball. Then I noticed the blue pillowcase my head was on. I sat up and pulled the case off the pillow, tossing it on the floor. I fell back down and closed my eyes.

Axel's lips touched my cheek. "I'll be back soon," he said.

I felt the warmth of the throw Axel settled over my covers, but I was still so cold—so damned cold.

Life's Fitful Fever

I woke up in the dark, tangled in covers. Sweating, burning, but still so cold.

"Axel?"

No answer.

"Axel?"

"What's up?" Axel's voice came from the other room. His head peeked in the door. "What's wrong?"

I felt so dizzy, and my heart was pounding. "I don't know. . . . I don't know. . . ."

He kneeled next to me. "Hey, it's okay. I'm here."

"Can you lie down with me?"

He hesitated for a second, then climbed under the covers, wedged against me, put his arm around me. "That better?"

"Yeah." There I was, bothering him again. But I was scared out of my skull to be alone in the blackness. "Wh-what did my aunt say?"

"Let's talk about this in the morning."

"Why? Was she mad at me?"

"No! No one's mad at you, Willow, except you. She was upset, but not with you."

"But I messed up her plans. . . ."

"Get out of here. That shithead was hardly indispensable."

"And now she has to deal with my crap. . . ."

"She *wants* to deal with your crap, Willow. She's your aunt. You'll see. You'll talk to her tomorrow."

I felt a hot, stinging pain in my chest and throat. "She's coming here?"

"Did you think she wouldn't?"

I didn't answer.

"Calm down. I can feel your heart racing, for God's sake. What do you think Agatha's gonna do, whip you?"

"She's gonna say what she always says, and right now, I really can't deal with the righteousness of it all."

"She's not a preacher. . . ."

"She could write scripture. The gospel of Agatha Moon. It wouldn't be a real effort. She could just write down whatever comes out of her mouth."

"Stop. You're not being fair."

"Oh, yeah? Well . . . fair is foul, and foul is fair."

"Hey, you stealing my Shakespeare quotes?" He laughed. "Are you going back to sleep, or what? Otherwise, I'll make us something to eat. You realize we didn't eat dinner?"

I realized a lot of things. Having missed a meal was the least of them. "I'm not hungry."

"All right, that's something else we need to discuss. You're turning orange from all the damn carrots you eat."

The tears started again. Who knew why . . . ?

"Hey, hey . . . don't start crying again. I'll leave you and your carrots alone for now; don't worry."

I sniffed. "How'd you know I was crying? I didn't make any noise."

"Your whole body got stiff. Believe me, I know all the signs of your crying by now."

I started sobbing.

"Oh, Jesus. I didn't mean. . . . Turn around, will ya?"

I shook my head no, pressed my hands against my eyes.

"Willow . . . I'm kind of used to only answering to my-self, being alone with my fucked-up thoughts. So if I say the wrong thing, you have to forgive and forget it, okay?"

I faced him, fat drops rolling down my cheeks. "I'm not crying because of you. I'm crying because of me."

He held his pinky against my cheek, let a tear land on it, whooshed it like a windshield wiper. "You're entirely too hard on yourself."

But nowhere near as hard as Aunt Agatha was going to be.

The morning had to come, and so it did.

Axel's stomach was churning. He got up to scramble some eggs. I asked for egg whites only, but he said no.

He watched me chew. Nothing to do but swallow the poison. I didn't eat the toast, but he didn't say anything about that.

153

I asked Axel if he would get me some clothes and my iPod, and to try and stall Aunt Agatha until the afternoon. It was like postponing my sentencing.

My thighs throbbed with every step, but I had to pull myself together to take a shower. I was overcome with the oily smell of Craig on me and felt like he'd smeared his grimy paw prints all over me. It was worse than the smell of puke, and I don't know how Axel could have lain next to me without heaving from it.

Left foot, right foot, left, right. . . . I tried to concentrate on walking, but the inevitability of the future kept forcing its way in.

Axel felt sorry for me, but that would pass. . . . He was going to come to his senses. He'd see that I wasn't worth the effort.

I made it to the closet. He'd said I could help myself to a T-shirt and sweats for after the shower, in case he wasn't back when I came out. I opened a built-in drawer and thumbed through the shirts, looking for what? I didn't know. They were mostly black, with a couple of navy blue thrown in.

That's what I'd become. Someone who couldn't choose between a black or a blue shirt that I was going to wear for ten minutes.

Black. Blue. Black. Blue. Black and blue. My mind meandered. . . .

They more I fought the memory, the more it surfaced. And so this minor decision became nearly impossible because my energy was channeled into blocking the pain.

Then I spotted something between the last two shirts:

a razor blade. I picked it up, fingered the sharp metal, pressed the dull edge against my fingers. I stared as though it would speak and offer some other explanation. But Axel used disposable razors; they'd been in the bathroom the other day. So what else would Axel need a blade for, besides coke?

I noticed that there was something on the edge. Brown flecks.

It looked like dried blood.

I remembered that night on the boat, before Axel put his T-shirt on. All those cuts. Did Axel slash himself with the razor blade?

Tell you the truth, if I'd had that blade handy the night before, I might have sliced into a vein or two myself. But bleeding to death seemed like a nasty way to go, if you thought it through. Why not take a bunch of pills and just go to sleep?

I put the blade back and took a black shirt.

Now I had something to discuss with Axel.

I found something else tucked on the side of the pants drawer. A photo of a boy, maybe five years old, in a blue suit. Brown hair, dimples. He looked kind of like Axel. Maybe a nephew or something. I stuck it back in and grabbed a pair of grey sweatpants.

I went into the bathroom and started the shower, waiting for it to get hot. I wanted it to scald, to burn away Craig's touch. If you boiled water, you distilled it, destroyed the toxins, making it pure. I wanted to distill myself.

Stupid, stupid, stupid. . . . Stupid and worthless.

155

The water was smoking, and mist filled the room. I climbed in.

Water pelted my bruises. They lit with fiery pain. I took it. I deserved it. I washed, scrubbed, and would have used steel wool if I'd had some. I thought of Craig behind bars, steaming, too.

I thought of his hand at my throat. I shoved the knob in to stop the water, grabbed the towel, pushed the terry against my eyes and cried again.

So much for the cleansing shower.

Finally, I dried myself off, brushed my teeth with the hospital toothbrush, and put on Axel's clothes. The pants were baggy, even though I pulled the string tight. *Whatever.*

I stepped out of the bathroom. Axel was back. He'd brought my whole suitcase. "Here. You look silly in my sweats. Like your mom bought you the wrong size."

I shrugged. *Who really cared, anyway?* I flopped onto a bench and slumped down against the table.

"How do you feel?"

"Like someone beat the shit out of me," I snapped.

"Okay, got it. Dumb question."

"No, it wasn't. I'm just a complete bitch. I'm sorry."

He slid next to me. "Listen, your aunt's coming in a few minutes—"

I tensed up. He put his arm around me. "Relax, okay? I told her you're gonna stay with me a few days. That's what took me so long, convincing her you'd be all right here. She just wants to see you for a few minutes."

He pointed to the counter. "Look. I even brought you your bag of carrots."

156

I leaned into his shoulder. "Why are you so nice to me?"

"Why do you ask? Can't you just accept it?"

I shook my head. "I keep . . . I keep waiting for it to end."

"What?"

"Your tolerance for me."

"It's not gonna end." He shifted the towel on my head, pecked the spot he'd uncovered.

Why, why couldn't I trust him? "Everything's so dark, Axel. . . ."

"It just seems that way," he said, rubbing his hand on my back. "If you lighten up . . . " His tone changed, taking on an almost scary intensity, and his hand tensed, pressing against me a little too hard. "If you lighten up, so will the world."

Interesting words from the guy with the bloody razor blade in his drawer.

"Hellooo, dear hearts." Aunt Agatha's voice catapulted down the hatchway.

"Oh, God," I cried. I realized I hadn't brushed my hair out or gotten dressed. The magnitude of these tasks, combined with Aunt Agatha's arrival, threatened to burst my brain.

"Come on in, Agatha," Axel called. His voice was back to normal. His hand loosened up, and he gave my back a final pat. "She loves you, Willow. She's on your side." He got up and leaned against the counter, like he was getting out of the way.

Aunt Agatha climbed down the steps and headed

toward me. She looked so sad. "Willow . . ." she said, hugging me. "Are you all right?" She tucked a strand of my hair, which had fallen out of the towel, behind my ear.

Hmmm . . . She sounded worried, not judgmental. I made myself look at her. "I . . . I guess."

"Scoot over, kid." She gave me a playful slap on the arm, which hit my bruise. I swallowed the pain.

"I was so stupid not to notice what was going on with that boy. It's been a long time since I was a teenager." She picked up my hand and kissed it. "Can you forgive me, love?"

Forgive her? It was all my fault.

I nodded anyway.

"This is going to be hard work, Willow. You're going to have to focus to clear your head of all this clutter."

Just when I thought things might be different, she was off on her mission and clutching my hand. All good lectures came served with a side of hand-clutching.

"Wipe your mind clean of it. Don't let it linger. Wallowing is the devil's tool."

Apparently I was to fear the devil, but I wasn't allowed to believe in a god on my side. Or was I supposed to think of her as God?

I felt like someone had shot me up with Novocain, big time.

"Dear heart, Axel asked me to let you stay here for a few days, so I will. He's a good friend, I can see that. So rest, but don't wallow. Don't cave in to the ego sickness. And when you return, we can move on with our work."

She gave an extra tight squeeze, like a big pinch. "Nothing can affect you unless you let it, Willow."

Besides everything else, my feelings were my fault, too.

"I've gotta go lie down," I said, pulling my hand away and getting up. "I haven't been able to will the pain out of my bruises yet. I need an hour or two more, I guess."

I went into the bedroom, pressed my head into the pillow, and tried not to made any noise while I cried.

I heard the door close. Great. *Was Aunt Agatha going to enlighten Axel about ego sickness now? What if he started spouting that stuff, too?*

I hoisted myself up and headed to the door, leaning my ear against it.

Axel said, "Agatha, with all due respect, is the word *tact* in your vocabulary?"

"Excuse me, darling?"

"Willow calls you a bulldozer. Get it?"

"Not really. . . ."

"You're plowing right over her."

"That's absurd!"

"Maybe, maybe not. But *she* feels that way. And she thinks you don't listen."

"I do. . . ."

"With your ears, but not with your heart."

Aunt Agatha didn't say anything. *She had to be getting pissed. What the hell was Axel doing?*

He continued, "What happened to Willow yesterday isn't something she can just forget. If she doesn't deal with it, it's gonna haunt her forever. You're telling her to repress her emotions, Agatha, and you're wrong."

159

"I'm not telling her to repress her emotions. I'm telling her to release them."

"But she can't just release them. Not everyone deals with things the same way. She needs to talk out her problems. She's already weighed down with so much shit from her mom . . . and now there's this."

There was another long silence. I both wished that I could see and was glad that I couldn't see her face.

Axel said, "Here's the deal. Willow needs you . . . and she needs you to listen. You telling her she's suffering from ego sickness makes her feel even worse. And it makes her resent you."

Why wouldn't Aunt Agatha speak? I wanted Axel to shut up already. *What if she changed her mind about allowing me to stay with him?*

But he didn't shut up. "I know you care about her. I told Willow that, but she sees you as an adversary. She's screwed up, lonely . . . and yet you're right there."

"You had to *tell* her that I care about her?" She sounded so hurt.

"Well, I mean . . . she knows you love her. But she feels trapped by the *way* you love her . . . like if she doesn't do what you say, you'll take your love away."

God, that was it! That was it, exactly.

I didn't even realize I was crying until I tasted the salty water dripping between my lips.

"So what do I do?" Aunt Agatha's voice cracked.

"Be there for her, with no comment. You can't control her."

"I don't mean to control her—"

"Agatha, I hate to tell you this, but it's controlling to tell someone how to think and how they should deal with their problems."

"Young man, you don't seem to know much about tact, either."

"I'm just talking to you like you talk to her."

He really did have a lot of guts, saying all that stuff. Or maybe I was just spineless for never having stood up to her. No matter how many times I tried, I'd always backed down.

Then again, I could never have described it. The pain. It was just too close to get a good look at.

There was more silence.

"No one's ever spoken to me like this," Aunt Agatha said after a few moments.

Uh-oh.

The silence grew so much that it ran out of space and slid under the door, rising in my face like a thick, maddening fog. I wanted to scream, "Say something!"

As if she heard my thoughts, Aunt Agatha finally spoke: "Thank you, Axel." Her voice was low and thoughtful.

I didn't know what to make of that. It sounded like Axel had gotten through to her, but I couldn't allow myself to believe that. Who needed more crushed hopes?

I felt all caught up in the swirling fog. Consumed. I made my way to the bed and closed my eyes.

The Doors

I woke to the sound of Axel's cello. Maybe it was my mental state, but I thought it was the most beautiful thing I'd ever heard. So pure . . .

I kept my eyes closed and let the music come for me. It was the first time I'd ever felt completely taken away by classical music. I'd always kept a little cynical piece of me in reserve, like a skeptic leaning against the wall with arms folded, saying, "Whatever." Now the music lifted me—all of me—to another place. A happy place.

Go figure.

The music stopped. The cello thunked as it was settled into its case, and then the latches clicked shut.

"Willow?" Axel was next to me. He touched my face. "Willow, you awake?"

I opened my eyes.

"I thought I saw you moving around. You feel any better?"

I shrugged. "I liked your music."

"Vivaldi," he said. "It's soothing. You were having a nightmare earlier. I tried to lie down with you, but you slapped at me, and . . . you bit me." He showed me the bruised teeth marks just below his thumb.

I gasped, horrified. *Talk about biting the hand that feeds you.* "Jeez, Axel . . . I-I don't know what to say."

He sat down, kept his feet on the floor. "It's fine. You do whatever you need."

"I certainly don't need to *bite* you!"

"Well, I just wanted to calm you down. So I figured a little Vivaldi might do the trick. To me, he's always been the bridge between the conscious and the unconscious, the conductor to sweet dreams."

"I guess you were right. The music really got me." I sat up and leaned against the wall. "That reminds me of something Jim Morrison said."

"Oh, great."

"Sorry . . . I didn't mean . . ."

"No, no. Go ahead. Tell me. I'm dying to hear ol' Mojo's sage words."

"It's about why they named the group 'The Doors.' He said, 'There are things known, and there are things un-known. And in between are the doors.'"

Axel ran his hand back and forth across the teddy bear throw. "Yeah, well, your friend Morrison used drugs to go through the doors of perception. That was his whole rap. Testing the boundaries of reality."

He traced the outline of a bear. "I do it with beautiful music."

"You *do* drink. . . . "

"I don't drink to enhance my thoughts. I drink to dull them," he said in a sharpened voice, with a hard stare.

Interesting distinction.

"It's funny . . . you know a lot about someone you can't stand to hear about."

He shrugged and looked down. His voice got soft and low. "My dad's friends' wives always went on about him. That's when I started to lose it a little. I mean, it was like they actually forgot I was me."

I lifted his hand away from its tracing, squeezed into it. "Axel . . . I'm really sorry. . . ."

"It's okay." He took his hand back, forced a smile. "What do you want for dinner?"

"Dinner? Didn't we just have breakfast?"

"You slept through the day. I was playing Vivaldi for hours."

"You didn't have to do that."

"Hey, I need the practice." He tousled my hair. "Oh, I almost forgot . . . I had one interruption. When I had to sign for this . . ."

Axel left the room and then tried to re-enter while carrying a big, fat stuffed penguin with a red bow. The bird was obese. It got wedged in the doorway, and Axel had to shove it through. "It was hell squeezing him through the hatchway," he said, balancing the penguin on my lap.

I hugged it. "Axel . . . it's the cutest thing I've ever seen! How'd you know I love penguins?"

"I could just tell." He sat on the bed's edge. "Only kidding. I'd like to say I'm psychic, but all they had besides him were teddy bears, and you weren't so thrilled with them on your throw."

"I *love* him!" I gave my penguin a peck.

"Read the card," he said.

"Waddle it take for you to feel better? Hope this flies. Love, Axel."

"I never claimed to write like Shakespeare," he said.

"I think it's beautiful. A little corny, but from the heart."

"Waddle you name him?"

"Okay, now you're pushing it." We both laughed. I regarded my new friend, tweaked his beak. "Hmm . . . he's paunchy, he looks like he takes himself way too seriously, and he makes me laugh. I'll name him Falstaff."

"I like a girl who knows her Shakespeare," Axel said.

"Thanks for this—and for everything." I moved Falstaff aside and hugged Axel. "Especially for talking to Aunt Agatha."

"You mean last night?"

"No, today. I heard what you said."

"You did? I closed the door so you wouldn't."

"I listened at the door. I thought Aunt Agatha was gonna give you a talking to. Anyway, that was nice, what you did."

"I had to make up for that dream thing. So am I upgraded from jackass status?"

I smiled. "Yeah."

"Good to see a smile. I haven't been doing such a good job with that, huh?"

"You've been doing an excellent job—with everything." I grabbed his hand again. "I don't know how I could have gotten through yesterday—"

"You don't have to thank me. I'm just grateful I walked in when I did." He kissed my forehead.

"So what was Aunt Agatha doing in there, while you were talking? She hardly said anything."

"She was doing shots."

He laughed at the look on my face.

"Jeez, just kidding! She was listening and considering, that's all."

"She's never gone that long without speaking. I thought she was getting pissed."

"No, she actually . . . she actually looked like she was gonna cry. She feels really bad."

"Huh."

He reached his hand like he was going to slap me on the leg and then stopped, probably remembering my bruises. "So, you want a bean burrito? I'm kinda hungry."

I shrugged. I really didn't want to eat at all. I knew I couldn't get out of it, though.

But the thing that had been eating at me needed to be voiced. "Axel, I have to ask you something."

"Hmmm . . . sounds serious. Do I need the vodka?"

"You may . . ."

He gave me a half amused, half nervous look and held my hand tighter. "Okay. . . . I guess I'll go get it if I have to. Shoot."

"I found the razor blade in your drawer."

His face went blank and pale. He pulled his hand away, got up, left the room.

In the time it took me to follow him, he was already sitting with his vodka at the table.

"Axel . . . I saw the blood on it."

He didn't say anything, wouldn't look at me. Just eyed the glass, tossing back three shots in a row.

"Axel . . . *talk* to me."

He didn't answer. Took another shot, slammed the empty glass down.

"I'm scared. . . . "

He focused on me. I never saw so much pain in someone's eyes. "I don't wanna go there, okay? Don't be scared, and don't worry about me. But I can't go there."

I wanted to do something. Yell at him, beg him, hug him . . . but I just nodded.

"Can you leave me alone for a few minutes?"

I nodded again and went back in the bedroom.

That went well.

❋

I didn't know what to do with myself. Between my own fucked-up life and Axel's apparently also fucked-up life, I could barely think straight.

Falstaff seemed to be glaring now, like he wanted to flip me the bird.

I sat on the bed and saw the towel lying between the pillow and the wall. It must have come off in my sleep. I'd never brushed my hair out, and now it was going to be one big, fat skaggy knot.

God, I really had no right to be a girl. I didn't dress the part, and I didn't act the part. I couldn't handle the simplest girly requirement. I couldn't even bring myself to put on makeup.

Unlike my mom.

That made me think of Saturdays with Mom. Every Saturday, it was the same thing. I waited all week for Mom to come home, and on Saturdays, I waited for her to take me out. To our big Saturday breakfast at the diner. The one time we sat across from each other at a table and could be together.

But to get to the diner, I had to survive an endurance test.

She rose leisurely, then had to sort through piles of clothes in her room and on the banister to find something to wear. Then came the makeup. The makeup was the worst. I couldn't believe how long it took her to put that brown base stuff on. She spread it around and around, smoothed it, dabbed at it. . . . Finally, it was time for the powder. How many times could she hit herself on the nose with a puff? Then the eye shadow . . . eyeliner . . . mascara.

It was lunchtime when we left to have our breakfast at the diner, to face each other without facing each other. Our standing appointment for talking about nothing.

It was always after one o'clock; you could count on that.

"Whatcha doin'?" Axel leaned in the doorway, looking stupefied.

Seeing him made me want to burst into tears. For him or me, I couldn't say. "Thinking about my mom."

"Yeah? What about her?"

"None of your business."

Gee, that wasn't nice, was it? I was mad at him, kind of. Because of the razor blade? Because of him not talking about it? Because he'd chosen to pickle his brain on vodka?

Because he was flawed? Was I that self-centered?

He nodded, unoffended. "Okay." He flopped next to me, knocking Falstaff on his side and firing vodka breath in my face.

"Do you mind . . . ?" I asked, waving the smell away.

He hiccuped. "Mind what?"

I sighed. "I can't deal with you drunk."

"I'm not drunk."

"No?"

"No. I'm impaired. There's a difference."

"Yeah? How so?"

"I can still perform most tasks, but with greater difficulty. It's a trade-off. Because the task of living becomes doable."

That would've been funny if I hadn't been crying.

"Aw, don't cry, Willow." He wrapped his arms around me. "I'm sorry I'm letting you down. Maybe you should go back to the barge. I'm almost positive Agatha's sober."

I cried even harder.

"Okay, okay. I'm an asshole. Please don't cry." He squeezed me tight. It hurt my bruises, but I didn't tell him.

"Oh, God, Willow, I wish I had what it takes."

"To do what?" I asked into his sleeve, my voice muffled.

"To . . . be." His voice had that intensity again, and this time it *was* frightening.

"To be what?" I asked.

"Just . . . to be."

169

A Walking Shadow

Axel released his grip, then got up. "Enough. I said I was gonna take care of you, and I am. Let's eat."

He nuked us bean burritos from the freezer and served them with salsa. I didn't know if he did it with greater difficulty or not. I'd never seen him nuke burritos before, but it didn't require much skill, anyway.

I picked at the filling and the salsa, leaving the tortilla part. Axel watched me eat.

We ate across from each other in silence. The mushy bean filling made my teeth feel like they were sinking into mud.

"Good?" he asked when we were almost done. His voice and gaze were steadier now. The food must have sobered him up somewhat.

I nodded.

"You wanna go for a walk?"

"I don't think so. My legs ache." I got up, headed back into the bedroom, and sat down.

Axel followed me. "How 'bout a game?"

"What?"

"Charades."

"I thought people played that in teams."

"So we'll be a team."

"But we're not playing against anyone."

"Then we'll definitely win."

He actually had a point. "Okay. You go first."

"This is a Shakespearean character," he said.

I rolled my eyes. *Big shocker there.*

Axel clutched at his chest, pretending to be mortally wounded. He staggered and swayed, dipped, and collapsed onto the floor.

"That could be almost any character from a tragedy," I pointed out.

He got up, grabbed the towel from the bed, draped it over his head, and then made stabbing motions against it.

"Polonius behind the curtain," I said.

"You got it. Your turn."

"This is a founding father," I said. I rubbed my mouth and made a face like I was in pain. I pointed to my teeth. Then I made a chopping motion with my hands.

"George Washington," Axel shouted.

"I cannot tell a lie. You're correct!" I said.

We played several rounds. Axel was a horse, a chair, Napoleon Bonaparte, and a midnight snack. I was a fish, a car, a basketball, and King Lear. (Hey, two could play at Shakespeare.) We played until our sides ached from laughing.

Then I had to sit down. Axel sat next to me on the bed.

Without warning, the sorrow ambushed me again, like

a highwayman lurking in the shadows of the road. I leaned my head on Axel.

He hugged me. "What's wrong?"

"It hurts so much." I grabbed up some of the fuzzy teddy blanket and twisted it.

"What does?"

I released the blanket, gathered it again. "Being me."

He kissed my forehead. "I'm here for you. You're not alone."

"I'm just a big piece of crap. Worthless." I twirled the material around, around, around.

"Don't say that. You're beautiful."

"Yeah, so beautiful that you couldn't stand the thought of being with me." I clawed at the blanket now.

"That's not true! I told you. . . . I couldn't do that to you. It's because of *me*, not you."

I was digging into the fleece, like I wanted to rip a hole in it. "You didn't want me because I'm"—the word was a torch setting fire to my insides—"fat."

"*Fat?* Jesus, Willow, a twig is wider than you. You're like a human toothpick." He stared at me with worried eyes. "Willow, you know you're super thin, don't you?"

I didn't answer. What I knew and what I felt were two different things.

"Hello?"

"Yeah," I said, through fresh tears. "I know I'm thin on the outside. But on the inside, I'm really fat."

"I knew you were starving yourself with those stupid carrots. Didn't your mom ever notice?"

I shook my head no, scattering tears.

"Your aunt?"

"She questioned me a little, but she kept letting it slide."

"Guess what? I'm not. Starting tomorrow, you're eating whatever I tell you to. Period."

"No."

"Yes."

My words exploded from my mouth. "They always picked on me at school, I was so fat. Now at least they leave me alone. Don't let them do it anymore, Axel. Please."

"Calm down. You're getting hysterical," he said, using my face as a water slide for his fingertips. "You can eat without getting fat."

"No, I can't."

I was trembling. The thought of going back to school like I used to be was too much.

"You're killing yourself, Willow."

"And you're not?"

He laughed—a strange, twisted laugh. "Not yet."

"What's that supposed to mean?"

"Relax. I was just kidding."

I wanted to believe him, but the tortured look in his eyes was no joke.

After all that, I was ready to collapse. It was like I hadn't slept at all, let alone slept the day away.

Axel looked pretty wiped, too. "You want me to lie down with you again?" he asked.

I nodded yes. "I'll try not to bite."

Axel shut off the lights. I crawled under the covers, and he followed, putting his arm around me. He made me feel safe, something I hadn't felt for as long as I could remember.

This was friendship, I realized. Being with someone you could argue with, confront, resent, bitch at, even bite on occasion. Someone who, at the end of the day, both literally and figuratively, offered you refuge against a brutal world.

I woke to the sound of a woman's voice in the galley, along with Axel's voice, which was mixed with confrontation and stress. He was asking her what she was doing there. Then the bedroom door shut again.

I thought about pressing my ear against the door, but it seemed wrong to intrude on whatever Axel was involved in out there. So I sat on the bed, listening to their voices without hearing what they said. Axel sounded very upset. Then I heard something fall. It sounded like the books stacked on the floor.

What the hell was going on?

Then there was silence. I waited a few minutes to make sure she was gone. Then I came out.

It *had* been the pile of paperbacks that fell. They were scattered around on the floor.

Axel leaned against the stove. His eyes were glassy, and he was wringing his hands. My presence didn't even register.

"Hey," I said. "You okay?"

He turned toward me, but kept his head down and said nothing. He kept wringing his hands. *What was wrong with him?*

"Axel . . . "

"Did . . . did you hear?" he asked softly. "Did you hear everything?"

I shook my head no, but I wasn't sure he saw it. "No. I didn't want to eavesdrop on you."

He let out a sigh, seemed to loosen at this.

"What is it, Axel?"

"Nothing." Finally, he stopped messing with his hands. "It's nothing."

I wanted to hug him, but there was this invisible wall around him now.

I bent and picked up *The Catcher in the Rye*, putting it on the table.

"Omelet?" he asked, still looking at the floor.

"Sure," I said.

He went to the cabinet, rattled some pots and pans around, and took one out. Then he opened the refrigerator and took out the eggs. He did all this without so much as a glance in my direction.

I stooped and began picking up more of the books.

Hearing a cracking sound, I looked toward Axel. He'd dropped an egg. Clear ooze seeped around the shattered shell. I thought maybe the yoke had survived whole, but a second later, orangy yellow slipped out from under the fragmented pieces, mixing into the ooze.

Axel dropped, just like the egg. He curled into a fetal

position on the floor, his arms buckled around his legs, his head buried against his knees.

His cries were high-pitched and disjointed. They came out in a jumble, then stopped, then erupted again.

I sat next to him, leaned against his trembling body, and put my arms around his waist. I had no idea what was going on, but whatever it was, it was bad. Really bad.

There was nothing I could say, so I said nothing.

Even though I held him, I couldn't get near him at all. He'd built a fortress around himself that was impossible to break through.

It was up to him to raise the gate.

Soul Kitchen

Axel lifted his head. His eyes were red. He stared ahead at his bookshelves, avoiding me.

The galley stank of the woman's perfume. My sinuses were clogged from it.

"She raped me," he said. His voice was flat, almost dead-sounding.

"What?"

"The woman who was here . . . Marianne . . . she raped me, when I was thirteen. I mean . . . you know . . . statutory rape." He stopped, swallowed. "It wasn't like . . . like I fought her."

"Who is she?"

"She's married to one of my dad's friends. A city councilman."

We sat there for a while, stewing on that revelation. Then he said, "After a few times, she passed me around to her girlfriends, too. Like some kind of X-rated Ken doll to play with."

"Oh, God, Axel. . . ." It all made sense now, Axel's reactions to my wanting to have sex, his trying to stop me, protect me. "Axel . . ." I held him close, and again, we sat without words.

Then he said, "I didn't think she'd show up here when I called her yesterday. I never dreamed she'd come herself." He had a bit of a coughing fit then.

I got up and got him a can of iced tea.

"Why'd you call her?" I asked as he sipped.

"I did it for your aunt."

"What do you mean?" I got some paper towels and bent down to clean up the egg.

"I asked her to do some fund-raising for Agatha. Go look on the counter. There's a stack of checks for her."

I finished with the egg. Then I picked the checks up from the counter.

The first one was for $5,000. It was payable to The Music Barge, Aunt Agatha's nonprofit organization. The second was for $3,000. The third was for $10,000. I shuffled through the stack. There had to be at least thirty checks, all in the thousands, all made out to the barge.

I checked the names on top. Mostly two names, husbands and wives. The signatures all seemed to be the wives'.

"What is all this?" I asked.

"Donations for your aunt's barge, to finish it. That's what rich folks do, to feel better about having so much. They make tax-deductible contributions. I just let them know, via Marianne, about the worthiness of Agatha's cause."

"How'd she get so many, so fast?"

"She probably worked a cocktail party."

I flipped through the checks. "Did you sleep with all of these women?" *Oh my God, did I really ask that?*

He shrugged. "Probably not all of them. I haven't looked at the names." He pulled himself up, leaned against the counter. "I didn't contact Marianne because of my history with her—though it helps that she owes me, I guess. That, and that I could technically have her arrested."

He shifted his feet and stared at them. He still wouldn't look directly at me.

"But really it was because she loves to climb up on her little soapbox and plead her case for her charity or arts organization of the month. She gets to be in the spotlight that way. So I knew she'd get the job done."

He breathed in and out deeply. "I just assumed she'd use a courier."

Another breath. "I told her to use one next time . . . a courier. I just . . . I just hope she does."

"You think she'll come back?"

"Let's just say Marianne can be a bit persistent. And she was awfully glad to see me. She backed me into that pile of books. . . . " He shuddered. Just then, he looked like a little boy, trying so hard to act tough, but not succeeding.

"You should have her arrested. You made me press charges against Craig."

He let out a weak laugh. "Willow, when it happens to a girl, it's sexual assault. When it happens to a boy, it's a rite of passage. It's a high five."

"She shouldn't be allowed to get away with it."

"The damage is done. And I'm sure my dad would be

less than thrilled with having his best friend the council-man's wife arrested for the rape of his son."

"Your dad wouldn't be on your side?"

He shook his head, still looking down. "No. No one would be on my side. There was no violence. No one held me down or beat me up. She said it to me just now, that I didn't seem to mind. I didn't. Until . . . something snapped."

"Where was your dad during all this?"

"He was always working or something. Not hanging out with me, that's for sure. I was raised by nannies. . . . I think the only criteria for getting their job was that they were hot."

"Hot?"

"Yeah. Dad found time to visit whoever my nanny of the month was, in the middle of the night. I heard them, sometimes, when I woke up, couldn't sleep, or took a walk around the house."

"That's disgusting."

"Yeah, well. It gets worse. Because dear Marianne wasn't my first. When I was twelve . . . one of my nannies . . ."

I was speechless, again. What could really be said about all this? I mean, besides all the moral crap he knew without me spouting it.

I kissed him on the cheek. "Axel, I'm gonna tell you what you keep telling me. It's not your fault."

"Thanks." He attempted to smile, but it looked more like a grimace. "The only problem is, it's not about guilt for me. It's about the weight. Life's just too heavy to bear."

I totally knew what he meant.

✖

We finally sat down to eat breakfast. Axel grabbed up the Caesar and Brutus salt and pepper shakers and chucked them into the trash without comment. I remembered he'd said they were a gift, and now I knew from whom.

I actually ate more than I wanted to—almost all of my eggs—because I didn't want to give Axel any more grief. He was really worried about me.

He drank a whole pot of coffee. I guess it was better than drinking vodka.

I was really worried about him.

Weren't we the pair?

Finally, it was time to tackle the hair. I thought about taking another shower, but the last one hadn't been so thrilling, so I figured I'd put it off another day and give the bruises a break.

I wet my hair, then went back in the bedroom and sprayed the heck out of it with the anti-tangle stuff. No more knots, it promised. Sure, all you had to do is actually comb your hair out sometime before it dried.

I managed to get the top layer smoothed before my arm bruises throbbed so much I had to stop. What lay beneath would have to stay unattended for now.

Then, I took off Axel's baggy clothes.

I was dressed in my own clothes, had semi-brushed out hair. . . . You'd think I'd feel better. I didn't. It just doesn't work that way.

Then there was a knock at the door. *Oh, good. What could it be now?*

Axel called, "There's a police officer here, Willow."

Fabulous.

"He's one of the guys from the other night, at the hospital. Can you come out?"

I could . . . but I didn't want to. Those cops saw me at the lowest point of my life, and I was only slightly higher now. The only person less desirable was Dr. Personality at the hospital. And Craig.

"Willow, did you hear me?"

"Yeah." I sat on the bed, trying to calm my speeding heart. There was no reason to be uptight, after all. Nothing was my fault, so how could anything bother me?

Yeah, okay.

"Are you coming?"

"Yeah."

I must not have sounded very convincing, because Axel said, "Can I come in there for a minute?"

"Yeah."

The door opened. Axel stepped in and closed it again. He sat next to me, put an arm around me. "It's not a big deal. He just wants to update you on what's going on."

"Is—is he out?" I didn't know if I wanted Craig to be out or not. I felt bad at the thought of him in jail, and I felt threatened at the thought of him out.

"No."

"He's been locked up all this time?"

"Yeah." Axel didn't seem too choked up about that. "C'mon, it'll take two minutes. You'll get some closure."

"Closure?" I doubted I'd ever close the door on Craig, but I got up anyway.

I didn't even remember the cop in the galley as one of the cops from the hospital. That's how messed up I'd been. He was young, in his twenties. Nice eyes, sympathetic. You'd think I'd recognize them, but I didn't.

"Hello, Miss Moon. How are you doing?"

I stared for a moment, holding back several sarcastic answers that came to mind. "Um . . . all right, I guess." *There you go.*

He smiled. "Glad to hear that."

So glad I could make you glad. That makes it all worthwhile. I must have been recuperating, because my inner obnoxiousness was making a comeback.

I just nodded.

He continued, "I'm here to inform you . . . " *Good lord, cops could be so formal!* "that Mr. Craig Culligan has entered a plea arrangement in the matter of his sexual assault on your person."

Okay, did we have to bring that up again? I knew why Mr. Craig Culligan had been arrested.

He went on, "Mr. Culligan is beginning his sentence of two to four years immediately."

"Two to four years?" I asked, shocked. "He's going to jail for two to four years?"

"Ma'am, the assistant district attorney felt that even though he had a prior record, in the interest of sparing you testimony—"

"No, no. I'm not complaining about too little time. I'm

183

saying . . . good God, he's going to spend the next two to four years of his life behind bars?"

"Yes, Ms. Moon. That's correct."

That had to suck. Had he really done something so awful to me that he deserved that? I had led him on . . .

"Okay, officer. Thanks for letting us know." Axel shook the cop's hand and sent him on his way, and fast.

Then he came over to me, lifted my chin, and stared into my eyes. Funny how he could do that when the pressure was off him.

"Don't you *dare* feel sorry for him. I saw you run for your life. Do you realize that?"

Big surprise, I was crying again.

Axel said, "Why is it you have compassion for him, but not for yourself? Aren't you allowed any sympathy?"

I didn't answer.

I didn't actually know the answer, but I suspected that it was no.

So I cried another river into Axel's shirt. It's a shame they couldn't collect my tears to use in the next water shortage.

I was just pulling myself together when we heard a knock at the hatch. Then "Helloooo, my dears!"

By now, my head felt like it was going to spin off of my shoulders. "Axel . . . "

He patted my hands. "She's gonna do better this time. You'll see."

I sat on the bench and watched Aunt Agatha prance down the stairs in her tattered, paint-splotched sneakers. She ran over and hugged me. "Willow, are things improved today?"

Did she want to hear the truth? *Oh, what the hell*. "Not really. Maybe a little."

"It takes time, sweetheart."

Did she really just say that?

She grasped my hand for a moment, then released it.

"I'm gonna go practice," said Axel. He went into the bedroom and shut the door.

Aunt Agatha seemed different, somehow. More relaxed. More allowing. Her whole body looked looser, and I swear to God, she was giving off this peaceful, forgiving aura. It was like one of those ocean waves subliminal tapes telling your subconscious over and over that things were going to be just swell.

Her eyes were full of sympathy. She said, "When you were two, you were afraid to be alone. I used to watch you, sometimes, in that tenement where you lived before you moved to Long Island. And you were terrified that I was going to leave. You must have been left alone at some point."

From the bedroom came the sound of Axel's stirring music. It sounded like his cello was crying.

Aunt Agatha continued, "You'd go to sleep clutching my hand through the crib bars. If I even moved my fingers, you'd wake up and cry. I sat there for hours, holding your hand. I'm willing to do that now, Willow, if you need me."

I let out a tremendous sob and fell into her arms.

185

Axel's cello cried, and I cried, and Aunt Agatha held me close.

She loved me, she really did. She loved me even though I wasn't perfect and even though I'd screwed up my life, couldn't wipe my mind clean, and I'd probably never be what anyone would describe as normal.

She wasn't going to leave.

"Do you want to talk?" she asked when I'd stopped.

"Not right now," I said.

"Whenever you're ready," she said.

"Thanks."

We listened to Axel play. "That boy is such a talent. I hope he decides to go to Juilliard."

"Axel's got a lot to deal with, Aunt Agatha. Just lay off him about Juilliard, okay?"

She sighed, then laughed. "I guess if I can learn with you, I can learn with him. We all need our room to breathe, I suppose."

I smiled. "Yeah, we do."

Axel's music was interrupted by a weird synthesized version of the opening of Beethoven's Fifth Symphony. "Da da da dum." Then at a lower pitch, "Da da da dum."

"What, pray tell, is that?"

"It must be Axel's cell phone," I said.

He came in a few moments later. "Agatha, I have fantastic news for you. I just got off the phone with someone at the mayor's office. I got you a berth."

"Excuse me, dear heart?"

"I got you a berth. It's in Brooklyn. Near the Brooklyn Bridge."

Aunt Agatha looked stunned. "How . . . "

"I know a city councilman."

"You know a city councilman?" Aunt Agatha stared at Axel and his straggly hair in disbelief.

"Actually, it was his wife who arranged it. She called the mayor's office, and they called me."

"A city councilman's wife."

"She owes me a favor."

"A city councilman's wife owes you a favor." It was a rare thing for Aunt Agatha to be reduced to repeating things.

He nodded. "At least one."

Aunt Agatha's mouth hung open.

"What's the matter?" Axel asked. "Is Brooklyn no good? I can push for Manhattan."

Her eyebrows raised. "No, no, Brooklyn's perfect. Better parking."

"Hmm, parking. I didn't think about that. I'll ask for a parking lot, too."

"Just who are you, young man?" She gave him a poke in the chest. "Are you putting me on?"

"Axel's last name is Ridge," I cut in. "His father is Wade Ridge."

Aunt Agatha looked Axel up and down as though she'd never seen him before. "My word . . . *the* Wade Ridge?"

Axel nodded.

"Your father has quite a reputation. They say he's invincible in the business world, godlike."

"He's something, all right," said Axel.

"My word," Aunt Agatha said again. "Wade Ridge. A city councilman's wife. My word."

"So it's cool?" Axel asked, probably trying to steer Aunt Agatha away from the topic of his father. "You're happy with the site?"

Aunt Agatha jumped up and embraced Axel. "It's cool."

"I've got something else for you, too." Axel picked up the checks and handed them to her. "Here are some donations for you to finish the barge and get the concerts going."

Aunt Agatha shuffled through the checks, color draining from her face. "Axel, my dear, I'm overcome. Why did you do this?"

"Well . . . I told Willow that I'd do the work on the barge, but I'm not all that good with a hammer. I might have set you back, like, ten years. Now you can hire a work crew."

She eyed the checks again. "I certainly can." She hugged Axel again. "Dear boy, you're a miracle. I don't know what to say."

"Just say thanks," I suggested.

"Evermore thanks, dear heart," Aunt Agatha said, squeezing Axel's arm. "Evermore thanks."

❖

Axel made more coffee, and Aunt Agatha hung out with us for a while. They talked about music. I sat next to Axel. Actually, I slumped next to Axel, elbows on the table, head in my hands. I was feeling a little light-headed, kind of zoned out.

I didn't know or care about the differences between

Bach's and Schubert's work. If they both sounded good, what else mattered? Personally, I'd rather hear Jim singing "Roadhouse Blues."

After about an hour, she stood and kissed us both. "By the way, Willow, I ordered you a new sofa, with a pull-out bed. It's being delivered tomorrow."

I bugged out at the news. I shook, and grabbed Axel's shirt.

This wasn't the reaction Aunt Agatha had expected. "Dear heart, what is it?"

"Axel has to stay with me, *please*."

She clearly thought I was losing it. "Calm down, Willow. We've put Axel out enough, don't you think?"

I wrapped my arms around Axel's neck like she was going to pull me away at that moment. "Axel, tell Aunt Agatha you want to stay on the barge."

He looked into my eyes. I was sure he knew the driving reason for my behavior.

I didn't want to be alone on that couch, it was true. And I was afraid of the dark—and the nightmares, too.

But the thing that scared me most was on the sailboat. It was that razor blade in Axel's drawer.

"Willow, chill out, okay?"

"Tell my aunt you want to stay with me."

He sighed. "Agatha, I don't want you to think I'm taking advantage of Willow or anything. . . ."

"No, no, darling. Quite the opposite," she said. "You've helped her through the hardest time of her life. But you have your own life—"

"I don't mind staying with Willow, as long as you're comfortable with it."

Aunt Agatha looked from me to Axel to me again. She said, "Willow, I won't pry your fingers loose from a hand that you need to hold. But you have two hands, and I hope you'll see your way clear to letting me hold the other one."

I let go of Axel, got up, and hugged Aunt Agatha.

"You can have my other hand." I said it low, practically whispered. "I was always . . . I was always afraid that my grip wasn't strong enough to hang on to you."

"Dear heart, we've suffered from acute failure to communicate in the past. But that *is* in the past now. Let the record show that I love you more than anything."

"I love you, too, Aunt Agatha."

"I'll see you both tomorrow," she said, offering a final wave. She pointed at Axel and said, "I expect you at sunrise, mister. Cello in hand."

Remembrance

"Feel better, now?" Axel asked.

"Much," I said.

"Good." He slammed his hands decidedly on the table. "Let's go celebrate."

That might be pushing it. "Where?"

"Chinatown."

"Chinatown?"

"Yeah. I didn't forget about your little eating thing." He wagged his finger in my face. "So if you want to watch over me—and I know you do—you're going to have to put up with my demands."

I hesitated about what to say. This was a possible re-opening of the razor discussion. But I knew he didn't want to go there, and hadn't he had enough anguish for one day? "What are your demands?" I asked.

"There's really only one—you have to eat. And I mean really eat, not just pick out a few bites of burrito filling. Chinatown is a good starting point. Okay?"

It wasn't. I was so scared to be a blimp again. . . . To

be on the outside how I still felt on the inside. I went over to a bookshelf and pretended to browse through titles.

"Willow, you need to gain some weight. But that doesn't mean you'll gain all the weight back. I promise."

"I'm afraid . . ." I pulled a book off at random, looked at the cover without looking at it at all. "I'm afraid that once I start eating, I won't be able to stop."

"You're a prisoner to food either way. Don't you see that? You need a middle ground."

I flipped through pages, not registering a word I saw. "There isn't one."

"Yes, there is. You'll see. For now, all I want is your word that you'll eat. Deal?"

I read the title as I re-shelved the book. *As I Lay Dying*—a title we could all identify with, in one way or another.

"Deal, Willow?" Axel repeated.

I didn't have a choice, did I? "Deal." I sat back down at the table. "How are we getting there?"

"Hank."

"Hank?"

"He's my driver, when I need one. My guy on call."

Well, la de da. "You have a guy on call? What does he do, wait around for you to contact him?" I hoped Hank had a few good books on hand.

"Nooo. He works for my dad, doing a bunch of things. One of his jobs is to be my driver."

Wow, this really drove home the class difference between us. It was forgettable on his small sailboat. "If you have a driver, why didn't you call him from the hospital instead of using the car service?"

Axel shrugged. "I didn't think you were up to Hank just then. He's . . . a bit talkative."

I stood. "Okay, well, you call Hank, and I'll go tell Aunt Agatha where we're heading. I have to catch her before she leaves."

"You all right, going out there alone?" He looked very concerned.

"Where . . . into the world? Yeah, I can handle it." I gave him a peck. "You're sweet, you know that?"

I hoisted myself up the steps. Had to do it sometime.

It felt strange to be out in the sun after so long. I shaded my eyes with my hand to have a look around. Then I headed down the ladder to the dock, feeling a jolt with every movement.

It hurt to walk at first. But step by step, I got used to the pain, and by the time I reached the parking lot, I'd forgotten about it.

Aunt Agatha was just getting into the VW. She got out again when she saw me. "Dear heart, what's wrong?"

"Nothing. I just wanted you to know that we're going to Chinatown tonight."

"You're not planning on taking the A train into Manhattan, are you? I'm afraid I can't allow that. It's much too dangerous."

"No. Axel's driver is coming to pick us up."

"Indeed!" She looked at her sad, beaten car. "In that case, maybe I should hitch a ride." She laughed. "Ah, well. Thanks for keeping me informed, love. And if there's ever an emergency, please call the theater. I don't care if I'm in the middle of the opening number—you're more important."

"Okay."

A florist's delivery truck with a Park Avenue address painted on its side pulled beside us. "Hey lady," the driver yelled out the window to Aunt Agatha, "you know the *Perchance to Dream*?"

"Darling, I don't go for all that brooding nonsense." She dismissed it with a wave of her hand. "In order to dream, one must awaken."

The driver gaped for a moment, then said, "Lady, you always talk like a fortune cookie?"

"Are you looking for the sailboat *Perchance to Dream*?" I asked him.

He smiled widely, no doubt grateful that I wasn't Confucius, Junior. "You got it."

"Is the delivery for Axel Ridge?"

He checked his chart. "Yup."

"I'll take it. I'm on my way there right now."

"Okey, dokey. Just sign here, please."

I signed, and I expected him to hand over roses, orchids, or maybe something really exotic. He was from Park Avenue, after all. But the thing he handed me was the most ugly, pathetic excuse for a floral gift I'd ever seen. It was less than a foot tall, with spiky green leaves sprouting from the branches that grew from a central trunk. It looked as pathetic as Charlie Brown's Christmas tree.

I hoped the delivery guy wasn't expecting a tip for bringing this thing, not that I had money on me anyway.

I handed it to Aunt Agatha as the driver backed out over the crunchy gravel.

"What *is* this nasty plant?" I asked her.

"It's rosemary, dear heart. It's an herb."

"You mean as in 'Rosemary, that's for remembrance'?" I remembered Ophelia spouting about it when she'd gone mad.

"Exactly. . . . But what's with all these *Hamlet* references?" Aunt Agatha scratched her head. "Is everyone taking arms against their seas of troubles?"

"I hope not," I said. I scanned the wrap for a card, but there was none. Really, it wasn't needed. The point was made with the gift. It was obviously from Marianne, and the message was to remember her. She had, after all, known about Axel's love for Shakespeare. She'd bought him the salt and pepper shakers.

"Listen, can you take this plant to work with you? Just give it to someone?"

"Why? Isn't it Axel's?"

"I can't explain, but Axel can't see this, okay? It'll upset him."

"Rosemary will upset him? How does he react to dill?"

"Aunt Agatha . . ."

"Dear heart, this is all fascinating, but I've got to get rolling. I'll give the plant away if that's what you want." She plopped it into the back seat next to her fiddle, which was good, since it wouldn't have lasted two seconds on the front seat with no back.

"Thanks, Aunt Agatha. And remember, don't tell Axel."

"I'll certainly never forget this rosemary." She slammed her door and turned the key. Her engine roared to life. "Toodle-oo, chum!" She blew me a kiss and took Marianne's poisonous gift back to Manhattan.

I could not believe that woman. Axel was right. She was persistent. I guessed she thought she'd get him back into bed if she kept up her pressure. What she was really going to get him into was a straitjacket. Or into the water, face down, like Ophelia.

I paced back and forth, ignoring my bruises, kicking into the gravel, and thinking. This was all my fault. Axel called Marianne to fix the mess I made.

Because of me, Axel was getting hit on again, and I had to help him.

But how?

While I was ruminating, a black limo pulled up.

"You must be Hank," I said to the stout, grey-haired guy who got out of the limo. His jacket was open, and I could see a gun holster strapped under it, resting against his shirt.

He squinted at me suspiciously. "Who wants to know?"

"I'm Willow—a friend of Axel's."

"Oh, yeah?" He smiled and extended his hand. I took it, and he shook it vigorously.

I winced.

"Y'okay there?"

"Yeah, I'm just a little banged up at the moment."

"I can see that. Ol' Axel didn't beat ya up, did he?"

"No."

"Yeah, I'm just teasing. That kid, he'd never hurt ya. Gotta love him. Now his big brothers, they'd stab ya in the back." He chuckled. "Just kidding—kind of."

I saw what Axel meant about Hank not shutting up.

"Well, let me go get him for you, then."

"Okay, young lady. I'll wait right here."

Axel was climbing off his boat when I got there, and we started back to the parking lot together. "I met Hank," I said. "How come he's packing?"

Axel rolled his eyes. "My dad's a security freak. He hires ex-cops so they can carry. He's got a few guns at each house, besides his insane security systems."

"You don't want a gun?"

"Do you *want* me to have a gun?"

Good point.

"But don't you want security?"

"The biggest threat to me is *me*. Should I wire myself so an alarm goes off if I get too close to myself?"

His little suicide jokes were a little too close to the mark to be funny.

"I don't like that kind of talk," I told him.

"I'm sorry." He sounded sincere. "That's just how I get by, making stupid jokes, even to myself."

I grabbed the bottom of his shirt and yanked it up. His chest looked worse than I remembered—littered with scars and more recent–looking, scabbed slashes. "I think you'd better try something else." My eyes filled with tears. "I wouldn't call this *getting by*."

I let go of his shirt and pushed past him, heading back to his boat.

"Willow," he called, "come back."

I turned around. "I'm sorry, but I can't pretend nothing's wrong. I can't make jokes about this. I'm so fucking scared for you." I was really creating a scene. Good thing it was getting late and no one else was around.

I thought he'd race past me, back to his boat and his precious bottle.

I thought I'd have to go tell Hank never mind.

Instead, he came over and hugged me. "You're right." His voice was so low I could barely hear him. "I know I have to deal with this. Just not tonight, okay? I can't take anymore for today. Please?"

I was sure that if he let go, I'd collapse from worrying. But I nodded.

And he didn't let go. He kept his arm around me, all the way to the limo.

A girl could get used to that, I thought.

The Lobsters

"What's the word, Hank?" Axel held the limo door open for me, then got in and slammed the door. The automatic locks clicked shut.

The inside was big enough for both of us to bunk in, and it was pretty darn comfortable, too. I wouldn't have minded dozing on those cushiony leather seats. They sure beat my sofa.

"Missed ya, kid. We all do. The old man misses ya."

"Yeah? He say that?"

Hank paused. "No."

"Didn't think so," Axel muttered.

"You know he's got problems showing how he feels," Hank said.

"Yeah. It's tough to express yourself when you're not actually there."

The limo pulled out of the boatyard driveway into Rockaway. What would people think when our homage to excess cruised by?

I was still checking everything out: the bar, the TV, the

DVD player, the telephone, and the surround-sound speaker system. It all seemed so over-the-top.

Axel reached toward the bar. "Could you please not?" I asked.

He leaned back, empty-handed.

"Thanks," I said.

"You know who misses you a lot is Walden. Asks for you all the time," Hank commented.

"Yeah?" Axel didn't seem too interested.

"Who's Walden?" I asked.

"Axel didn't tell you about his little brother?"

Little brother? "No, he didn't," I said, giving Axel an inquiring look.

Axel sighed. "Hank, I don't feel like chatting right now, okay?"

"Jeez, kid, I don't see you in how long, and this is how you act? Me and you used to be real tight."

"Yeah, you were the only one who would talk to me," Axel said. He sounded like he was getting tense. I patted his leg.

"Actually, I have a headache," I said. "Maybe we could just listen to some music?"

"Sure, sure," said Hank. "Take a look through the CDs. See whatcha like."

Leather squeaked as Axel shifted around. He leaned back and looked up at the ceiling.

I slid open the compartment of CDs and flipped through them. Surprisingly, there was a decent selection of rock and roll. They even had a Doors CD—*LA Woman*—but I couldn't put that on.

I took out a Vivaldi CD.

Axel smiled at the sound of the opening notes. He put his arm around me. "I feel like we're kind of reversing roles," he said, stroking my cheek. "I'm supposed to be taking care of you, remember?"

"Can't we take care of each other?"

"Hmmm . . ." he said, sliding lower on the seat and leaning his head against me. "I guess that could work."

The surround-sound made me feel like I was there in a concert hall with the instruments, like they were playing all around me. It may have been excessive, but it was great.

Axel was breathing deeply. I looked at him. His eyes were shut.

I gave him a kiss on the forehead and went to sleep, too.

Axel's sitting on a bench in his galley. He's staring at his chest and has the blade in his hand. He first runs the edge lightly over the skin, almost tickling, but rougher. He raises goose bumps.

Now he presses the blade in slightly as he strokes, cuts into flesh, welcoming the pain. Needing the pain.

Axel needs to bleed, and watches with deep fascination as the blood dribbles from the shallow cut, then flows when the blade re-enters, plunging deeper.

He needs to bleed. Needs the pain.

He lifts his wrist, examining it as though he's never noticed it before. He puts the blade to it, gliding it across, back and forth across the surface.

He takes in a breath and plunges the blade in harder, deeper. . . .

❂

"Willow, wake up!" Axel was shaking me, and he was a little rough about it.

"What, what?" I tasted tears when I spoke, and I could feel the wetness on my face. I was gasping for breath, and my heart was doing a triathlon.

"You were having a real freaky nightmare. You were flipping out. You woke me up with a jab to the head."

I was trying to calm myself as he spoke, trying to catch my breath. I breathed in and out slowly without saying anything.

There was a black plastic shield up, separating us from Hank. Axel said, "I raised the partition so Hank could concentrate on driving."

"Was I that bad?"

Axel nodded. "You fought me again when I tried to hold you and when I woke you up. That's why I had to shake you so hard."

"You can hold me now," I said, realizing that I was trembling. The dream had been so real. "I won't fight you."

He pulled me up against him. I lay my head against his mutilated chest.

"It was Craig again," I lied.

"Yeah? That explains why you were calling out my name." He ran his fingers through my hair. "I'm sure Hank thinks I beat you, now."

"I'm sorry, Axel. I can't control my dreams."

"I know," he said softly, sifting through strands of hair. "Sometimes I think I can't control anything about my life at all. I'm just a poor player, strutting and fretting. . . ."

The partition whirred down. "We're here," said Hank. "How's it going back there?"

"We're okay now, Hank," said Axel.

Yeah, we were just perfect.

There was a fifteen-minute wait at Wo Kee's, a small, bustling restaurant on Grand Street. The air swirled with chatter, clanking dishes, and an assortment of pungent aromas. The scents of hot and sour soup, pepper steak, pork fried rice, chicken and broccoli in garlic sauce all mingled in the air around the families and friends seated at red-clothed tables topped with tacky plastic flowers in equally tacky vases.

We stood by the gurgling fish tanks. A lobster at the top of his heap caught my eye. He seriously looked like he was waving at me with his rubber-banded claw.

"You like lobster?" Axel asked.

"How can you eat something that's eyeing you?" I said. There had to be fifteen or twenty lobsters piled in there. *Did they know what they were in for?*

"Wanna watch me?"

"Axel, that's horrible. Do you know they throw them into boiling water alive? And that they cry?"

"Oh my God . . . you're like the ultimate bleeding heart, you know that? My father would make mincemeat out of you."

"I never said I could make it in the corporate world," I said, tapping on the glass at my new friend, "nor would I want to."

"I can't believe you're bonding with the catch of the day. Do you, like, go to farms and play with the cows and pigs before they're slaughtered?" he teased.

"Axel, he winked at me, I swear," I said, pointing at the lobster.

Axel sighed. "You're gonna dwell on crustaceans all night, aren't you? You're gonna stare at them from across the room."

"Excuse me, table ready," the guy with the menus told us.

"Listen," Axel said to him, "how much for all your lobsters?"

The guy looked at Axel like he was nuts. "Why you want all lobsters?"

"I want you to give them back to whoever delivered them to you and have them set free."

"Free?"

"Yeah, back in the ocean."

"That make no sense."

"All the more reason to do it," Axel said. "So how much?"

The guy scratched his head. "We charge seventeen nine-nine each lobster dinner."

"Fine."

"But people want lobster dinner now."

"Tell you what, I'll give you double for each one." He pulled out his credit card, slapped it into the guy's palm.

The guy gave Axel another strange look—like maybe Axel stole the credit card—but then he seated us. He gave us our menus and hurried off, probably to tally up the lobsters and charge Axel's card.

"That was cool, Axel. Thanks."

"You do realize that they'll probably just get caught again eventually."

"Maybe, but you gave them a second chance—a fighting chance. Maybe they'll avoid the traps next time."

"I think you're giving lobsters way more credit than they deserve. They're not really like that one from *The Little Mermaid*, you know."

"Duh! He was a crab, not a lobster."

Axel laughed and spit out a bit of the noodle he'd been crunching on.

"Anyway, thanks for making me feel like we saved them. Gee, this dinner's costing you, like, $500 before we've even ordered anything."

"Yeah, I know. Next time, we go vegetarian. Or to a steak house. It's too late to save anything in there."

"Okay, gross!"

We checked out the menus. "What are you having?" I asked.

"I think I'm gonna have one of those lobsters I just paid $500 for."

I gave him a nasty look.

"All right, just kidding. Why don't we get a few dishes to share, and try 'em out?"

"Okay. But I don't wanna eat any meat. I can't, after all this."

He was willing to humor me. "We'll get tofu or something, then. We need some protein."

"Well, aren't you Mister Square Meal."

The waiter came, and Axel ordered six vegetable dishes with different kinds of sauces. Some came with rice, some with noodles. He requested no cornstarch or MSG with anything. The waiter nodded his head a lot, real curt. He said "Um-hmm" every time Axel ordered a dish, before Axel even got the words out—like he already knew what we wanted, but was being forced to go through this formality. He grunted when Axel finished. "That all?"

"That all?" Axel repeated. "We're getting six dishes for the two of us. You think we need more?"

The waiter gave Axel a dismissive brush of the hand, which I gathered meant no, and walked away.

"Nice attitude," I said.

"Whatever." Axel unwrapped his chopsticks, separated them, and started tapping out a rhythm on the table. "The food's excellent here."

I looked across at my lobsters, to make sure no one was trying to cook one.

"So, you interested in hearing about my little brother, or are you too fixated on your friends over there?"

"I didn't think you wanted to talk about him."

"Listen, I'm not gonna fall apart constantly, okay?"

"That's good to know. After all, when you do, it takes away from my time getting upset."

He reached across and took my hand. "You're gonna be fine, you know that? You're gonna rise above all the crap with your mom, and . . . everything else."

"Really? It's nice that someone thinks so."

"You don't need anyone's help but your own to get through it all."

"Is this your way of cutting me loose?" I asked.

Meanwhile, some kid with curly red hair a couple of tables away started screaming about an egg roll: *I want an egg roll now!"* His mom said, "You have to eat your soup first." "Nooo!" he hollered.

Axel went on. "I just want you to think about that when you're back home in the fall."

"Yeah . . . if I have a home to go back to. Maybe Mom will replace me permanently with Steve."

"It'll all work out. You've got your aunt, and she's not gonna let anything happen to you."

Now the kid flung his cup to the floor. Soup splattered all over his mom. *"No egg roll!"* she yelled at him. Then she yanked the hysterical kid away from the table, toward the rest room. *"Egg roll! Egg roll!"* the kid blathered.

I watched the little feet in sneakers being dragged off. "I know," I said.

❋

Our heaping plates of food came. Axel told me that without the cornstarch, it was much healthier to eat. Under Axel's close supervision, I took some of each dish.

He was right: the food there was excellent. Of course, given that I was used to making a meal out of raw carrots, I probably wasn't the best judge of any cuisine. I tried not to think about the calories I was consuming.

"Eat a noodle or two, will ya?" he asked.

I ate two noodles, then returned to the vegetables.

Axel sighed. "Well, at least that's a start."

"Okay, so tell me why you failed to mention your little brother to me."

"Well, it's funny," Axel started, then took a sip of his iced tea.

What's funny is that usually when someone starts off that way, what follows is almost never funny at all.

He went on, "That kid loves me so much, but mostly he just pisses me off. I mean, I care about him and don't wish him any harm, but he's got everything I always wanted. My dad never gave two shits about me, but he does all kinds of stuff with Walden. I know it's not Walden's fault, but . . . "

"Is that the boy whose picture is in your drawer?"

"Yeah. I see I have to be more careful in giving out invitations to borrow clothing. You really went sifting, huh?"

"I didn't mean to. . . . I couldn't focus and just kept pawing around."

He waved his hand indifferently. "Doesn't matter anyway."

"I didn't mean to invade your privacy—honest."

"It doesn't matter."

I leaned forward. "Okay, then. What does matter?" I asked, very seriously.

He shrugged and toyed with his chopsticks. Then his eyes got watery. "Nothing matters," he said, looking away.

"That's not true, Axel."

"If you say so," he said, staring off at the swinging kitchen doors.

"Axel, if you can be so confident about *my* future, why can't you be about your own?"

But he didn't answer me. He just kept looking somewhere off in the distance.

After about a minute, he turned back to face me and returned to the beginning of the conversation, as if he hadn't gone to wherever he'd been in his pain, ignoring the path our conversation had taken.

"My dad got married again, six years ago. His wife's real young, of course, and gorgeous. She wanted a baby, and along came Walden. Dad went back to the 'W' names, I guess 'cause the philosophy thing didn't work out all that well."

Our charismatic waiter dumped a silver tray in front of us, with the check and two fortune cookies.

"Go ahead, pick one," said Axel.

I tore open the plastic wrapper and cracked the cookie open. I read my fortune to Axel: "You are almost there."

Did I miss something? Where was I going?

Axel's fortune read, "An ounce of gold cannot buy an ounce of time."

"No kidding," he said, tossing the slip aside. "Someone should tell that to my dad."

 What Dreams May Come

Axel called Hank on his cell to pick us up out front, while I wished the lobsters good luck and bon voyage. We walked to the corner with our shopping bag full of leftovers. We passed electronic toys clanging and beeping at vendors' outdoor tables, ice being poured at the fish market, and people yammering all over the street. In the midst of bright multicolored restaurant and store lights, we were silent and dim.

We really knew how to have a good time.

Axel stopped right before we got to the limo. "Hey, thanks."

"For what? Eating?"

He laughed. "Yeah, but that's not what I meant."

"Then what did you mean?"

"Just . . . thanks." He hesitated for a moment, staring at me, then gave me a quick peck on the lips. It was enough to send my mind spinning.

He grabbed my hand and pulled me toward the limo.

"You guys have fun?" Hank asked as we slid onto the smooth leather.

Axel and I eyed each other. "You know, Hank, I don't think we did. I think we're gonna have to try again," said Axel. "Head over to the Village, okay?"

"Where you got in mind, kid?"

"Starry Nights."

"You got it," said Hank.

"What's Starry Nights?" I asked.

Axel patted my hand. "You'll see."

Greenwich Village was this cool, happening, kind of whacked part of downtown New York City. It had this feeling of diverse pieces clustered together and working in harmony. There was something in the air there—a buzz of excitement, a vibe that attracted all kinds of people, all mingling together. You could wear a suit, tie-dyed jeans, leather, or next to nothing, and it was all good. There were funky shops to explore—something Aunt Agatha and I used to do a lot on Saturdays when I was younger—and all kinds of restaurants and cafes. Starry Nights turned out to be a cafe.

There were tiny, sparkling, celestial-looking white lights strung all around the canopy, windows, and doorway. Axel led me inside, to more lights twinkling all across the ceiling and along the walls. It was like we'd entered the heavens.

The room was kind of dark. The strands gave off the only light other than the candles flickering at each small, round table. That really made me feel like I was in the night sky, surrounded by stars.

Conversation hummed, jazzy instrumental music played softly, and the smell of coffee beans wafted through the room. It wasn't crowded—about half the tables were filled. The hostess seated us near the darkened stage and handed us menus. "Sherrie will be out shortly," she said.

"Who's Sherrie?" I asked Axel.

"She's the singer here. Wait 'til you hear her." Axel grinned mischievously and added, "Of course, she's not as good as you are."

I blushed, remembering my one night of drunken superstardom. I swatted Axel with the menu, then opened it. "So what are you having?"

"Cappuccino and triple chocolate cake. How about you?"

I shrugged. "Juice?"

"Get out of here. You don't come to a cafe and order juice!"

"Tea?"

Axel sighed. "Try a cappuccino, will you? I think a good shot of caffeine will do wonders for you."

I made a face. "I don't like the taste of coffee."

"This is different. The foamed milk makes it smoother. Plus, you can sweeten it up with sugar." Noting my reaction, he added, "Or in your case, Sweet'N Low."

"If you say so."

"And have a piece of angel food cake. It's out of this world!" He laughed at his little joke. I didn't.

"No, thanks."

"C'mon. It's low fat." Half of Axel's face glistened in

the candlelight. It made him even more appealing and mysteriously sexy.

How could I refuse? "Okay."

While we were ordering, the stage lights came on. There were more sparkly lights, but also spotlights beaming down. Then a blonde in a shimmering white dress that kind of matched the lights slunk up to the mike. The pianist struck some introductory notes, which I recognized as the opening to the song "Someone to Watch Over Me." It was from the Broadway show *Crazy for You*. I knew it well, because Aunt Agatha had played that show and brought me the CD.

Then she sang. Axel was right. She *was* good. Haunting, even.

He touched my hand. "Are you up to dancing?"

Looking into those eyes, I was sure gonna try.

We were the only ones on the dance floor, and although I didn't really know how to dance, I wasn't self-conscious at all. Axel held me tenderly against him. Having his strong, warm arms around me was like being wrapped in a cocoon, safe. We swayed, taking baby steps.

The song was about how this woman was waiting for the person to arrive who'd take care of her. It was sooo appropriate for us, considering how we were watching over each other.

We were alone, despite all the other people in the

room. That dance floor became the sky, and we were moving among the stars. Nothing back on Earth could touch us.

As the song ended, Axel's lips hovered near mine. I thought he'd kiss me again. But then his lips grazed my cheek. I didn't take it personally this time.

Axel whispered to me in the dark when we were back on the sailboat: "Thanks, Willow."

"For what?" I asked.

"For . . . for being with me today."

I felt his hand trembling against my back. I rolled over and held it. I was thoroughly awake, thanks to the caffeine.

I held his hand tight and stroked his arm with my free hand.

"Axel . . . "

"I'm sorry. . . . I wish I hadn't laid so much on you." I could hear it in his voice that he was fighting tears. He went on: "I just haven't opened up in so long . . . it's like I couldn't hold it back anymore."

I moved closer to him, realizing that there was no way I could protect him from Marianne. I knew that only he could help himself through this, and all I could do was warn him so he would be prepared for next time.

"Axel . . . you were right about her. About Marianne. She's not finished yet."

"What? What are you talking about?"

I took a deep breath, exhaled, and told him about the

rosemary. When I finished, he laughed. "You think it's funny."

"The part with Agatha is," he said. "The rest, not so much. Marianne always did have a flair for the dramatic."

"What are you going to do about her?"

"I don't know. Ignore it for now. Once she's done getting the money for Agatha, I can tell her off or something."

"Or something?"

"I'll tell her off. Period," he said. He gave me a squeeze. "That was cute, you trying to shield me from her insidious plant. But don't worry, I won't bite into the poison apple."

"That's good."

"You sound surprised."

"I guess I was worried . . . that you might decide to take the easy way out."

He got up, got out of bed, turned on the light, and paced the cabin. After a couple of rounds, he asked, "And that way would be?"

To go back with her. Or worse . . . to use that razor blade again. But I couldn't voice these thoughts. I was too afraid of them.

"Axel, you said it yourself, when we first met. We're kindred spirits. We understand what it's like."

"What *what's* like?"

"To be so incredibly sad that you'll do anything to escape the loneliness."

"Yeah." It was a whisper; his voice was barely there. Then he stopped pacing. He was turned away from me, facing the closet.

I went on: "That's why . . . that's why I was with Craig."

"I know."

"My mind . . . it's just so dark in there sometimes. It's like a forest. I keep looking for the light. I thought that if someone wanted me, accepted me . . . then I could accept myself. The other night, I wanted to give up. . . . I wanted out completely. You knew—you held onto me so tight. You knew."

He didn't say anything.

After a moment, I continued, "But I don't want to die, not really. At that moment, it seemed like I did. But when I think rationally about it, I'm terrified of death. It's—it's even darker than life."

Still, he said nothing. His shoulders were slouched, his head bowed. I could feel his defeat just by looking at him.

Finally, he turned around. He looked directly at me, seeming deflated no longer. It was quite a transformation. Then he asked, "What do you think now? About how to get away from the loneliness?"

"I—I think I need to like myself. But I just don't know how."

"Why don't you call that counselor? I still have her card."

I considered that. *She did seem okay, even though I was nasty to her.* All I said was "Maybe."

He sat back down and took my hand. "It'd be a start, Willow."

"What about you, Axel? What's your way out?"

He stared at the floor. "I . . . I haven't figured that out yet. That's another reason I came here."

There was something about what he said that didn't sound quite right. Maybe it was the way his voice was shaking. I squeezed his hand.

"Axel, can we talk about the razor blade?"

"No." He still wouldn't look up and meet my gaze.

"Why not?"

He wriggled out of my grasp. "Drop it, okay?"

"I can't," I pleaded.

He faced me. His eyes seemed hollow, like something had gone out of them, leaving them empty. He spoke now, his voice flat and lifeless.

"It's just . . . it's just another way for me to handle the pain. I control pain that way, when I give it to myself."

"Axel . . . " I was trying to think of something to say. But what do you say to something like that?

"I'd rather punish myself than have someone else do it."

What did that mean?

"Why do you have to be punished at all?"

He shrugged. "Let's go to sleep. I have to practice with your aunt at dawn." He got up and turned off the light, then climbed back under the blanket.

"Good night, Willow." He flopped down on the bed with his back to me.

I lay there in the dark, trying to sleep. But I was terrified about what he'd said and even more concerned about what he hadn't. It hung in the air, waiting.

217

After a lot of tossing around, I leaned against him, reaching over to take his hand. I circled his wrist and then slid my fingers down to his hand, feeling something rough and raised along the way. It was a thin line, like a healed cut.

What if my dream was right?

Sick with worry, I finally fell asleep, clinging tight to Axel.

Their Exits and Their Entrances

I woke up, sort of, when Axel tried to get free of my grip. "No . . ." I cried, half asleep.

"I have to go meet your aunt, Willow. Let me go."

"Axel, Axel . . ." I moaned through the fog in my mind.

"Willow, let go. I don't want to hurt your bruises."

What he was saying finally registered, and I released him.

"Axel . . . "

"What?"

What could I say? We stared at each other for a long moment.

"Well?" he asked.

"Nothing. Never mind. See you later," I said, rolling over.

Axel went off to the barge with his cello, but I couldn't go back to sleep. I needed to think of a way to help him.

He needed more help than I could give him—that was clear.

What if I could get him into therapy?

Maybe I could get him to go if I agreed to speak to that rape crisis counselor. Maybe we could make a trade, a bargain.

Or I could tell Aunt Agatha. But what if he got angry? I sure did when he talked to her about me.

I must have dozed off, because suddenly a voice was calling my name.

"Willow?" Axel was shaking me.

I sat up, blinked, and rubbed my eyes.

"I hate to wake you, but . . ."

"What now?"

"Someone's waiting on the barge for you."

"Who is it?"

"Um . . . it's your mom."

"My *mom!*" *Jesus, was there no end?* "What's she doing there?"

"I don't know. . . . She said she wants to talk to you."

"God—you told her I was here?"

"What did you want me to do? Tell her you ran off to Antarctica with your penguin?"

"Oh, shit! I just don't need her drama on top of everything else."

"She didn't seem too dramatic to me."

"Yeah, that's her big act. She's all nice to everyone else, and they all think I'm crazy. They don't know what she's like."

"Well, she's here. So do you want to go there, or do you want her to come here?"

I grabbed Axel's arm. "Does she *know*?"

"I don't think so. . . . How could she?"

"Maybe the police called her . . . or Aunt Agatha. . . ."

"No. Agatha would tell you first. And we put Agatha down as your guardian on the forms. I doubt they'd call anybody else."

"I hope you're right." I took a breath. "Okay. I guess . . . bring her here. I haven't been back on the barge since— since Sunday. I can't deal with going back there *and* her at the same time. And can you get Aunt Agatha to come with her, too?"

"Sure."

While Axel went to go get them, I got dressed. I wasn't as freaked out about Mom as I normally would be. I was already numb from Axel's revelations.

After I was dressed and cleaned up, I sat at the table, waiting. Then Axel climbed back on the boat and came into the cabin. Aunt Agatha, who gave me a big hug, came next.

"Don't worry, love. She's not that bad today," she whispered in my ear.

Then came Mom, clomping down the galley steps in her clogs. She always wore clogs, whether they were in fashion or not. Usually, they weren't.

She also wore her usual humongous straw hat with a scarf tied underneath her chin and her oversized black sunglasses.

As Aunt Agatha always said, The Contessa had arrived.

"Willow," she said. That's what she always said. Never

221

hello or anything. Like *how are you* might kill her or something.

"Hi, Mom," I said.

She sat down next to me and planted a cold kiss on my cheek—and I do mean cold. Her lips and skin were always chilly. It was like her blood didn't run warm like everyone else's.

She smelled like a big ol' vitamin. It made sense that she excreted the smell. She took, like, thirty supplements a day. She was practically a slave to her vitamin schedule. It was funny how she could keep track of all that but somehow couldn't remember to pick me up from school until I'd been waiting for hours with the custodians.

"I met your boyfriend on the barge," she said, talking about Axel like he wasn't standing right there, only two feet away.

"He's not my boyfriend," I said.

"Hmpf," she said, meaning that she wasn't surprised.

"So what's up, Mom? How's Steve?"

"That's what I wanted to talk to you about. Can we have a little privacy?"

I looked at Axel and Aunt Agatha, then back at Mom. I really wanted to say no, but why subject them to Mom's theatrics?

"Fine," I said, getting up.

She followed me into the bedroom. At least I had Falstaff, my faithful but silent companion. He seemed to be appraising Mom from his perch on the bed.

The best way to handle Mom was to expect nothing. Because that's what I usually got.

"Well?" I asked. "What is it?"

She slid off the sunglasses and gave me her "pathetic" face. Except she looked slightly deranged with all that sunscreen caked on her skin.

"Steve left."

"Really?"

"Don't sound so happy about it."

I tried to wipe the smile from my face.

"He said I needed help."

No kidding.

"So I went to see a psychiatrist. He prescribed some medication."

"Seriously?"

Wow. What do you know? Steve wound up being a blessing in disguise.

"Yes. And so, since I've been on the medication, I've realized that I acted . . . shall we say *erratic* in the past."

I nodded. *Understatement alert.*

"So what I'm trying to say is, when you come home, I'm going to try—I'm going to try to be a better mother to you."

All right, that was reaching. I mean, nature was nature. But still, if she wanted to try . . .

"Would you like to say something to me?" she asked.

I wanted to say a lot of things to her, but she probably would've slapped me.

"No."

"How about you'll try harder, too?"

I narrowed my eyebrows. "What do I have to try harder

at? I'm always there, aren't I? When I'm not thrown out to make way for boyfriends, that is."

"That's what I'm talking about: your surly attitude."

Again, I could have said a lot to her. Like the fact that she was the one who'd made me this way, who'd shaped my attitude. Like the fact that it was more of a defense mechanism than a weapon against her. Like the fact that I'd love to let my guard down, but who felt like having her trample me one more time?

But I didn't say anything because frankly, I had other things on my mind. Like the fact that a guy had beaten and almost raped me. Like the fact that my best friend had a habit of cutting into his chest and wrists with a razor blade.

With all that going on, dealing with Mom would have to be on hold until September. I could hardly wait.

"Let's talk about it when I come home" was all I ended up saying.

"I thought I'd bring you home now. After all, you whined so much about leaving. By the way, that boy out there looks so familiar. I can't place him, but . . ."

"I can't come home right now. Aunt Agatha needs me."

"You didn't believe in Agatha's project when you got here."

"Yeah, well, consider me converted."

She pouted. "I thought we could spend some quality time together before school starts."

Yeah, me, you, and your makeup, I thought.

"I'm not coming home, Mom."

"And what if I insisted?"

I crossed my arms. "I'm not coming home, Mom. I'll see you in September, just like you wanted it in June."

She gave out a deep sigh. "Fine."

"Are we done here?" I asked.

"I suppose," she said.

"'Kay, then." I brushed past her, heading for the door.

"Willow?"

I sighed. "Yes?"

"Are you going to give me a chance?"

Oh, for God's sake. She wanted more attention. Meanwhile, she hadn't said a word about my bruises.

"Yes. Okay? I just have a lot going on right now."

"I'm going to need your help, too."

Yeah, what else was new?

"Everything will be great, in September. We'll have our own nirvana."

"Nirvana. That's one of those bands in your room, isn't it? I think that boy looks like one of those people in your posters. Is he in Nirvana?"

"No, he's not in Nirvana. Axel's not in any band. He plays the cello." I really didn't feel like getting into it all with her.

"You're kidding."

"No, I'm not. Aunt Agatha thinks he's excellent."

"With that hair?"

God, she was so fucking judgmental in her huge hat and clogs.

"What the hell does hair have to do with playing the cello?"

225

She gave me her most sanctimonious look. "Nothing. Nothing at all."

"Well, he *is* good."

"I'm sure."

She was so *not* sure, with that tone of hers. *Whatever.* I had no time for *that* trap.

"Good to see ya, Mom." I swung open the bedroom door, then sat down at the galley bench again.

Mom followed me out into the galley. "Are you sure I can't convince you?"

"Ciao, Mom." She loved to speak Italian, but she hated it when you beat her to it.

"Arrivederci, Willow," she said, giving me another frozen peck. She nodded to Aunt Agatha, then gave Axel a funny look.

"Maroon Five?" she asked, bringing up another group that she thought Axel might play in.

"Good-bye, Mom."

"Matchbox Twenty?" She tried again.

I shook my head no.

She started clonking up the steps when something occurred to me.

"Hey, Mom. You never knew any of the names of groups before. And you never looked at my posters. You barely came into my room because you couldn't stand all those *freaks*, I believe the term was. So what gives? Have you been hanging in my room?"

She turned with a kind of guilty look. "Well, Steve liked to listen to your stereo."

Yuck! "Mom! You had sex in my bed?"

Holy cow, I couldn't believe I'd blurted that out. But I really couldn't believe what had gone on in my room.

She didn't deny it! I thought I might hurl.

"I expect a new mattress, comforter, pillow, sheets . . . the works!" I shouted after her.

Axel looked mortified at the whole conversation. Aunt Agatha looked like she was going to burst with the laughter she was holding back. And Mom looked strangely proud of herself as she clonked on the last step and went out.

"The Doors, Mom. He looks like the guy from the Doors. It's the biggest fucking poster in my whole room," I hollered after her, just to show that I knew more than she did about my posters.

"And I want a lock, too! With a dead bolt!"

Those were my parting words. I must have turned completely purple. At least that's how I felt.

"You shouldn't allow her to get to you like that," Aunt Agatha said.

"Oh, my God! She had sex on my sheets! That's so gross!"

"You have a point," she said, obviously remembering her promise to listen without comment.

"Well, dear heart, I've got to go back to the barge. I've got a few people working there, thanks to darling Axel." She blew him a kiss. "I have to show them a couple of things, then head out for my matinee."

We both stood up, and she gave me another hug. "The couch is being delivered today. Will you two come tonight? I miss you, love."

"Yeah, we'll be there," I said. "Right, Axel?"

227

He nodded.

She started up the ladder. "Toodle-oo, chums."

"Bye, Aunt Agatha."

Axel gave her a wave.

"So what did your mom say?" Axel asked, when Aunt Agatha had left.

"Her boyfriend's gone, and she's on medication. She wants to be a better mother to me."

"That's cool."

"Yeah, except she didn't notice anything was wrong: she didn't notice my bruises, and she didn't even ask how I was or what I'd been up to all summer. All she wanted was company now that Steve's gone. She just came to get me for companionship. My name might as well be Lassie."

He laughed. "Sit, girl, and I'll make us something to eat. But sorry, but I'm fresh out of kibble." He laughed again and went to work at the stove.

Soon he turned back to me, saying, "Close your eyes." Axel was holding a plate behind his back.

"Why?"

"Just do it!"

I heard the sound of plate meeting table. "Okay," he said.

I opened my eyes and found a big steaming smiley-faced pancake looking back at me.

"Awww! How cool is that?" I was truly touched. My mom hardly ever made me breakfast, let alone anything like this. "Thanks, Axel."

"It's a reminder for *you* to smile." He sat with a stack of pancakes for himself. "And I see that it worked."

"Why don't you have one?"

"Who makes themselves a happy-faced pancake? That's borderline pathological."

"Then *I'll* make you one." The bench scraped as I pushed it back and stood.

"No, no. Yours will get cold."

"I don't care. Your pancakes sat while you made mine, didn't they? And I just can't be happy alone." With that, I put my hand to my chest and belted out a Broadway show song I hadn't thought of in years. It was called "I Want to Be Happy," and it was about the person singing not being able to be happy until the person they were serenading was happy, too.

Good lord, I couldn't even blame it on alcohol this time. Something about Axel made me sing.

"O-*kay*. Go ahead, then. I can't argue with that," Axel said, with eyebrows raised.

I dished the eyes, nose, and mouth out on the griddle with a spoon. So far, so good, considering I'd never actually made a pancake before.

"Where'd you learn that showstopper?"

"My aunt played in a musical a long time ago—*No, No, Nanette*. I used to listen to the CD over and over, when I was, like, eight. Would you like to hear the "Where Has My Hubby Gone Blues"?

"I'll pass," he said with a laugh.

I poured the rest of the batter around the face. It stayed

round—except for the right upper corner, where the batter veered out of bounds. Way out of bounds.

I served Axel his grinning pancake. A frown might have been more appropriate, with that huge lump on its head. It was like someone had bonked it good with a hammer.

"Sorry about that."

Axel smiled. "It's perfect."

We were kicking back, eating pancakes and joking around, when Beethoven's Fifth rang out from Axel's phone.

He looked at the number on his cell. His face clouded. He didn't have to tell me who it was.

"Don't answer it," I said.

"I have to." He flipped the phone open. "Yeah," he said, down an octave. He mouthed "be right back" to me and climbed up to the deck.

I sat and swirled pieces of pancake through syrup on my plate, waiting. But Axel still didn't come back down. *What were they talking about?*

Finally, I went topside to check on him.

Axel was leaning against the outside of the railing, staring out at the water. He was in exactly the same spot where I'd seen him when I first arrived at the boatyard.

That bitch had drained the life right out of him, quicker than any blade ever could.

He didn't see me coming, and when I touched his

shoulder, he flinched. Then he turned around and fell into my arms.

There was so much I wanted to say. But sometimes silence says it all.

The barge loomed across the water from us. Ugly memories sprang into my mind: being beaten and throttled on the couch, coming within seconds of violation, thinking I was about to die. . . .

We just stood there, silent on the deck in the sun, our skin baking and our insides raw. It felt like hope was the only thing left to laugh at, and I doubted Axel had the strength for even that.

"I told her not to call again," he finally said. "But I don't know if she'll listen. It's all just a game to her."

He was right: she was the cat, and he was the mouse, cornered in his hole.

"I still say you should tell someone. . . ."

"Forget it. That's not how it works in my world," he said sharply.

I pulled away from him, wounded by his harsh tone.

"I'm sorry, Willow. Let's . . . let's just forget her. Let's just let her go, and then she won't be able to hurt us. Okay?"

I nodded, wanting so badly to accept that this strategy could work.

"Leave her to heaven, huh?" I asked, even though I was hoping for the other place.

"Exactly," Axel said.

To Thine Own Self

26

"Here's the deal," I told Axel. We were back in the galley, where I was cleaning the dishes. He was just kind of slumped at the table. I went on: "I'll talk to that counselor if you go to therapy."

"I don't know. . . ." I could barely hear him over the running water.

"Axel, what's not to know? You said you needed to deal with . . . your problem." I clinked a dish against another as I put it in the rack, because I was busy looking at Axel.

"I don't feel like talking to anyone—" his voice broke off.

"We're all hurting, Axel. There's no shame in showing where you're wounded." I shut the water and started drying.

"Okay, okay. I'll make some calls tomorrow. Find myself a head-shrinker. Happy?"

"Yeah." And I was.

I took a shower, and then we headed off back to the barge. Axel carried my suitcase and a duffel bag with his stuff in it slung over his shoulder. We left Falstaff behind to act as the official watch-bird of the boat.

As we rounded the dock and got closer to the barge, I started to feel like things were flying around and around inside my stomach. Not butterflies, but bigger. Like bats, maybe.

I stopped walking.

"What's the matter?" Axel asked.

"I thought I could go back, but . . ."

He dropped the bags down and hugged me. "You're not alone. I'm here."

"I know . . . I'm not being rational. And Craig's in jail, for God's sake."

He rubbed the back of my neck, trying to calm me down.

"What happened to you was irrational. It's only natural that your response would be irrational, too. You just have to go in there and conquer the fear. Once you do that, you'll feel better."

I took three huge breaths in and out.

"Okay."

We went to the ladder. I hesitated, then climbed up slowly. When I got to the top, I suddenly felt dizzy and nauseated. It felt like ten years for Axel to inch his way up the rungs with the bags. I glanced from the top of the ladder to the door and back repeatedly and kept imagining Craig busting through the door.

Finally, Axel was on deck. "You all right?" he asked. "You look about ready to collapse."

"Let's just get this over with," I said.

I linked my arm with his, and he opened the door. Of course, the new workmen hadn't left a light on and it was pitch black, as usual. I had to let go of Axel so he could put his bag down and leave it with my suitcase by the door.

My heart started doing the mambo. Then I latched onto his arm again, and step by step, we felt our way in the dark to the lamp by Aunt Agatha's cot.

As soon as he flicked the light on, my eyes went right back to the scene of the crime. Sure, there was a brand-new sofa bed there now, but that didn't block the hideous memory. I saw Craig's red, angry face. . . .

Axel noticed right away. "Hey, hey, you feel like you're registering an earthquake of 10 on the Richter scale," he said as he held me close.

"Close your eyes," he said. "Just focus on me, not him. He can't hurt you now."

I squeezed my lids so tight I saw a kaleidoscope of colors and shapes.

"How's that? Any better? " he asked.

"Oh, yeah. I'm in a colorful earthquake now."

He laughed. "Look, I mean . . . no, don't look. I'm gonna carry you to the couch. You can just relax and not even open your eyes at all—not until you're ready."

"Will you lie down with me?"

"That was the idea of me coming, wasn't it?" His lips pressed on my cheek. "I'm here for you."

He lifted me, and I wrapped my arms around his neck and held on. We weaved through the piles of construction debris and materials until we got to the back of the room near the sofa bed. Then he put me down.

"One sec. I'm gonna open up the bed."

I couldn't bear to look. I just waited, eyes shut tight, and listened to the hinges doing their work.

"Okay." He lifted me up and laid me on the mattress with my head against the pillow.

He took my sneakers off and dropped them onto the floor, and then I heard him drop his own. The bed squeaked as he climbed on and put his arm around me. "How're you doing, Willow?" he asked.

My heart was halfway to my throat, and my pulse was racing. But Axel was so sweet that I just said, "Good."

"Liar," he replied.

"Axel . . ." I wanted to tell him how wonderful he was, how much I appreciated him, but nothing would come out. My expanding heart might have blocked my vocal cords.

"Shhh, I know. You don't have to say anything. Just relax and let your mind float."

I floated with it, right off to sleep.

The next thing I knew, it was morning. Aunt Agatha and Axel were playing music together again. So I took a chance and opened my eyes, and it really wasn't so bad. It helped not being on that horrible couch, and with the side doors of the barge both open, the place was flooded with morning sunlight that brightened the entire chamber. What a difference light made.

And there was that beautiful music; it cleansed me and soothed me as it swirled through my soul.

I got up and maneuvered my way over to them. It was awesome how they made something so difficult seem so effortless, their playing so perfectly meshed. For an instant, I regretted giving up the violin, but only for an instant. I knew I could never do what they did—let the music flow like that. I just didn't have it in me, couldn't feel what they did.

I loved watching their expressions as they bowed: they went from smiling to deep concentration to sheer amazement—like they discovered something new as they played.

But even more than that, I envied their partnership. They were on a musical journey together, a thrilling ride I couldn't share.

"Good morning, dear heart," Aunt Agatha boomed when the last notes faded and I'd applauded their work.

"Hey," Axel said with a sly smile.

"Morning, guys," I said.

"Feeling better?" Axel asked.

"Yeah," I answered, and it actually was the truth.

"Axel, would you be a darling and get us some coffee and rolls from the delivery truck before the construction crew arrives? Willow, did you bring your carrots?"

"Willow's been off the carrots, Agatha," Axel said. "Doesn't she look good, now that she's been eating a little more?"

"My, my. Yes. You do look healthier, love. I'm so glad. I just didn't know how to talk to you about that. You were so adamant about those carrots."

I shrugged and looked down. This talk about my eating habits was making me think about gaining too much weight.

Axel must have sensed it. He said, "You want me to see if they have a fruit cup, Willow? I know a buttered roll is just too far for you to go just yet."

"Yeah, okay. Thanks, Axel."

He headed off.

Aunt Agatha looked into my eyes and asked, "So, Willow, how are things?"

"Well, to tell you the truth, last night was really, really hard. I kind of freaked out when I got here. Axel—he really took care of me."

"I'm so glad you have him, dear heart."

She sounded so sincere. And knowing how much she liked Axel, I almost poured my heart out about him. But I didn't. It felt like I'd betray him if I told her what I knew about his past.

"How did it go with your mother? I ran out so fast yesterday, I didn't get a chance to ask you."

I told her all about it.

"Do you think you'll be all right there in September?"

"Do I have any kind of a choice?"

"You can always come live with me. I feel that you're old enough to decide what's best for you. And I'm buying a house in Brooklyn to be near the barge. If things get bad with your mother, you'll always have a haven with me. And even if they're good, which I certainly hope they will be, I hope you'll come visit me on weekends and in the summer."

Amazing. I actually *did* have a choice. I felt so light

now, knowing I could get away if that was what I wanted—or needed—to do.

"May I give you one piece of advice?" Aunt Agatha asked.

I nodded, quite happy to be asked first before she made a suggestion. This really was a whole new side of my aunt.

She said, "Always cultivate your garden."

"Huh?" I'd never had the slightest inclination to plant anything, so I didn't know what she was getting at.

"What I mean is, no matter what your mother says or does, no matter how she tries to manipulate you or convince you to do things her way, you have your own garden, your own patch of earth in this world. You can let in or keep out whoever you want.

"Fill your garden with flowers, trees, bushes, vegetables, whatever you like. It's your spot and your place in the sun. Take time to weed, take time to sow, and you'll reap life's finest rewards—on your own terms.

"And dear heart, the same applies to me as it does to your mother. If I act bossy or push you around, you have the right to expel me from your garden. It's yours, not mine. I might forget that sometimes, so don't be afraid to remind me."

I hugged her tight. "Okay. It's a deal."

That's when Axel came back, and it was just as well that he'd missed all the talk about gardens, figurative or not. He'd found me a cup of cut up melon, and he handed Aunt Agatha her roll and coffee.

We were just finishing our breakfast when five big

guys came in, all wearing work clothes. Three were middle-aged, grey, and beefy. But the other two were close enough to Craig in age and studliness to send a shudder through my heart. I edged my chair closer to Axel's, as close as I could get without ending up on his lap.

Aunt Agatha introduced us, then directed them to their tasks.

"So what do you think, kids? We're on our way, thanks to you, old boy!" She said this standing behind Axel as she squeezed his shoulders. "Are you two going to stick around today?"

"Maybe we could paint outside for a while," I said, needing to keep my distance from the workers, at least for the moment.

"Fine with me," Axel said. "But I have to make a couple of phone calls first. I'm gonna make your appointment, too, okay?" he asked.

"Okay," I agreed.

I'd been painting on the back deck for half an hour when Axel came back from his calls. "It's all set. You have an appointment tomorrow at noon."

"And you?"

He looked past me, at the water. "I found a therapist near where you're going. I can walk there, actually, so Hank can drop us off together."

"Oh, Axel. I'm so glad." I gave him a big hug, but he

was kind of stiff. I guessed that the thought of therapy was still making him nervous.

But I was sure it would help him.

It had to.

The Course of True Love

August was quite an improvement over July. Going to counseling helped. It made me feel so much better. Outwardly, my bruises healed, and I was on the way there on the inside, too.

My counselor, Jamie, found me a therapist in the Five Towns who I could start seeing in September, when I moved back to my mom's.

Axel didn't talk about his therapy, but he kept on going. That, to me, was the main thing.

Marianne never called back, at least as far as I knew.

And Aunt Agatha and I talked about my problems. I mean, we really discussed them. I didn't expect to iron everything out overnight, but I just wanted her to allow me my feelings. And to my surprise, she did.

Meanwhile, Axel and I divided our time between helping Aunt Agatha and just relaxing and unwinding. We talked, read books, and managed to have some laughs.

We went to the city a lot, first on therapy days, and then more and more often.

We did all the touristy stuff, like Madame Tussaud's wax museum, where we checked out everyone from F. Scott Fitzgerald to the Dalai Lama, all in wax. I told Axel he should have worn leather pants and stood really still in the rock and roll section. People would have started taking pictures with him, sure he was the wax Jim Morrison.

We went to the Museum of Natural History, where we hung with the dinosaurs, and to the Metropolitan Museum of Art, where we sat in the middle of the Monet room and marveled. We found out we both loved Monet, and Axel's aversion to plants, luckily, didn't extend to paintings.

One night, we were headed down 34th Street, toward the Midtown Tunnel. At least, that's where Hank was trying to drive. We were stuck in a tangle of traffic, behind a crosstown bus spewing grey exhaust, right in front of the Empire State Building.

"I've never been there," I said.

"Let us out, Hank," Axel said. "We're goin' up."

We stared at the dazzling city from behind the tall, elaborate sky deck fence on the observation deck of the sky-scraper. No one was taking a plunge off that roof. And there had to be at least a million lights up there. And probably a million more in Times Square alone. I was captivated by the tiny cars moving through the streets; they looked like they were moving through a maze, trying to zigzag their way out.

"It really makes you think, doesn't it?" I asked Axel.

"About what?" he asked.

"About all the lives, all the people out there. So many people crammed together in one place. How do they all get by?"

"I don't know, and to tell you the truth, I have enough trouble figuring out how I'm gonna get by, let alone anyone else."

"Yeah. It's interesting, though. I feel like if all those people out there can find their way, I will, too."

Axel shrugged. "Whatever works for you. . . . You wanna see where the barge's berth will be?"

"Sure."

We walked around the sky deck to the section facing downtown on the east side. He pointed through the metal. "See the third bridge? That's the Brooklyn Bridge. Your aunt's berth is just to the right of the bridge."

I grabbed onto the cold silver barricade, peering through it intently. "Cool."

I turned to Axel and took his hand. "I don't think I ever thanked you for doing that for Aunt Agatha."

"You didn't have to. Agatha still thanks me every day!"

"Axel . . ." The honking noises below suddenly seemed loud.

He studied me. "What?"

"If I didn't know you and someone described you to me, I don't think I'd believe them."

"Too fucked-up to be true?"

"You can joke all you want, but you are the most incredible, giving person I've ever met."

The air was cool up there. A chill ran through me, and I shuddered. Axel pulled me against him.

"No, I'm not," he said, running his free hand up and down my arm to warm me. "You and Agatha just happen to bring it out in me. I feel like giving to you."

"Some people never feel like giving anything to anyone. But you, you've given me—" I stopped, afraid I was going to cry.

He gave me a shy smile. "I feel the same way about you."

We held hands in the night sky, watching the twinkling lights just beyond our reach, just past the looming silver barrier along the ledge. We watched all the cars carrying people trying to find their way and the skyscrapers filled with people trying to get by.

It was dark there in our corner of the sky deck, but I wasn't alone.

I was no longer alone.

It was one of those "Duh, why didn't I think of this sooner?" moments.

"You know what we should do?" I asked, giddy with my realization.

"What?" Axel asked, looking up from *The Taming of*

the Shrew. We'd just finished working—stripping wood these days—and it was chill-out time.

I put *Pride and Prejudice* down on the arm of the sofa. "We should go see Shakespeare in the Park!" Every summer, Central Park features a Shakespeare festival. How perfect was that for Axel?

"I don't think so," Axel said quietly, shifting his position on the couch.

"Why not? Of all things I'd think you'd love to do . . ."

"Nah."

"*Nah?* That's not an acceptable answer," I said, crossing my arms.

"It's—It's the park," he said.

Ahhh, the park. I hadn't thought of that. "Have you talked to your therapist about not wanting to be near foliage?"

He fidgeted, staring at a cocoa-colored strip of mahogany that was propped against a sawhorse, finally saying, "Haven't gotten to that yet."

"Well, I think we should go. Just like I had to climb back onto the barge . . . you need to embrace nature."

"I don't want to, Willow." He sounded so sad—back to being an abandoned, hurting boy.

"Axel . . . you're punishing yourself over and over by denying yourself things you love."

"I don't love plants."

"Even if that's true, you do love Shakespeare."

He didn't say anything else, just stared at that piece of wood.

"How about we both do something brave? You know how I'm terrified of painting the roof? I'll do it."

He turned my way. "You're willing to do that for me?"

"It's for me, too. Aunt Agatha's right—we should face adversity, not run from it."

He thought for a moment, then nodded. "Okay," he said.

❊

So then I actually had to do what I'd promised—paint that horrific roof.

The next morning, we stood before The Utterly Vertical Ladder—as Aunt Agatha called it. I called it The Steel Terror, because terror is what struck me when I even thought about climbing it. Fastened flat against the outside wall of the barge, that ladder went straight up to the roof.

Axel went up first, carrying the red rust-resistant paint, rollers (which he'd somehow convinced Aunt Agatha were our friends), and a paint pan. Then he leaned over from the top, waiting for me.

I hoisted myself up, feeling the cold steel under my hands as I moved from rung to rung. Everything was going well—that is, until I looked down.

Axel groaned. "Why'd you do that, Willow?"

I didn't know. It was just in my nature to look back at where I'd been.

And now I was totally panicking. I froze right where I was, partway up the ladder.

"C'mon, you're almost there. Hey, wasn't that in your fortune cookie?" He smiled reassuringly and held out his hand.

I closed my eyes for a second. But when I opened them, I was still stuck right there, in the burning sun, on that infernal ladder. "Axel . . ."

"You can do it." He gave me a bigger smile.

I thought about Aunt Agatha's words when I'd crawled across the plank that first day. I put my mind in the soles of my feet and didn't worry about them meeting the rungs. I just had to know that they would.

At the top, Axel helped me over the ladder. "Whatever you do, don't look down from up here," he ordered.

"'Kay."

It wasn't that bad up there. As long as I stayed away from the edges, I could pretty much forget that I was on a roof. But still, I stayed close to Axel—just in case.

We got down to the business of painting, sitting on our heels and inching in patches across the long hot roof. Even with the rollers, it would take forever to finish. Still, it was cool the way the paint spread so smoothly over the metal. It made me feel like I could smooth other things over, too— like I could just roll right over my problems.

Axel and I were so intent on our painting that we rolled right into each other, painting each other's knees a deep red.

"Hey," I said. I bopped him on the nose with the roller, leaving a nice red dot.

"Hey," he said, bopping me back.

We were ready for the circus—or to guide Santa's sleigh.

He laughed, then guided his roller across my shoulder.

I returned the favor on his.

Then he pushed me down gently and painted me from

my neck to my ankle with his roller. It tickled, and I giggled like a lunatic.

Then I did it back to him. He actually kind of let me.

We rolled around the middle of the roof, swiping at each other with our rollers.

"Hey, kids, what's going on?"

I was perched over Axel trying to strike, but he had me by my wrists. We stopped wrestling and looked at Aunt Agatha guiltily.

"Dear hearts, perhaps you misunderstood. The idea is to paint the roof, not each other." Then she laughed. "You'd better start applying turpentine before you dry completely and end up needing to scrub with a wire brush. And whatever you do, don't light any matches while you're doing it."

It turned out to be a long, stinky process, cleaning ourselves off with turpentine-soaked rags. We held our breath as much as we could while we rubbed, but we had to breathe sometime and those nasty fumes stung. When we were finally finished, we looked like we'd applied some sort of bad henna treatment to our skin. Aunt Agatha promised it'd wear off eventually.

Hank picked us up and gave us a funny look. "Strange tans," he commented.

Axel and I eyed each other and laughed.

"You get the tickets, Hank?" he asked.

"Yup. I did."

"So what are we seeing?"

Please don't let it be Hamlet, I silently prayed.

"Romeo and Juliet."

"A tale of star-crossed lovers," said Axel.

"More like family-crossed," I said. "Didn't you ever feel like slapping those Capulets and Montagues?"

"Uh, no," Axel said. "And I hope you can refrain from those hostilities tonight."

"I'll do my best."

It was a beautiful evening to be outdoors. The temperature was at that perfect spot between warm and cool, and the park air smelled of grass and pretzels. Kids were shrieking with glee in the playground we passed, as they went flying on swings and slipping down slides. We held hands and walked among the tall trees toward the theater.

"You okay?" I asked him.

"Yeah, I am, actually." He smiled. "I'm feeling pretty good."

"I'm glad, because I was hoping I wouldn't have to return the favor and carry you through the park with your eyes closed."

He laughed, pulled me to a stop. "Thanks for getting me in here. You were right. I was punishing myself."

Again, our lips came so close, they almost joined. Time seemed frozen as he paused, breathing heavily. I knew he wanted to do it, to kiss me. *Really* kiss me. But he just couldn't, somehow.

I wanted to kiss him, too. All I had to do was move forward a fraction of an inch. But it might as well have been a mile.

He who hesitates is lost. Aunt Agatha was right again, damn it.

He ran his fingers through my hair, pushed some back behind my ear, and stroked my cheek. "I'm sorry, Willow . . ." he whispered, leaning his forehead against mine.

"Don't ever be sorry," I told him. "You've given me everything you could."

We headed down the path arm in arm, farther into the park.

The show was about to begin.

After the applause ended, we milled onto the path with the crowd, then sat on a bench to let the chattering people pass. Neither of us liked walking in groups.

The park had a different look in the lamp-lit night. It was kind of enchanted, like maybe your fairy godmother might decide to pop in and stir up some magic.

The temperature had gone down, but it was still comfortable, not cold. There was just the slightest breeze, a reminder that at any moment, Mother Nature could make you wish you'd brought a sweater.

"So, what'd you think?"

"It was even more beautiful to see than read," I said. "But so sad!"

"Yeah, fate sucks, doesn't it?"

"What do you mean, 'fate'?" I asked.

"Well, like I said before, it's a tale of star-crossed lovers. They were doomed from the very beginning."

I shifted my position to face him, leaning my elbow on the bench back, with my leg still on the seat.

"So you think they couldn't have done anything to change the outcome?" I asked.

He shrugged. "They tried, didn't they? It still didn't work out."

"Maybe if they'd tried something different . . . like telling their families to go fuck themselves?"

"Yeah, I wonder why Shakespeare didn't use that line."

"I'm serious here. Those feuding fools were the problem, not fate. Look how easily they forgot their differences when they found Romeo and Juliet dead. Why couldn't they work it out sooner?"

"Because it wasn't in the stars."

I swatted the idea away with my palm. "People cause trouble, not stars."

Axel focused on one of the tall metal lamps glowing onto the path.

"Axel, you don't really buy into that predestination crap, do you? Like we're puppets or something?"

He looked at me, his eyes shimmering in the lamp's beam. "Or something."

"Get out of here. Then what's our motivation for doing anything—for trying to get anywhere in life—if we have no control?"

He lowered his stare to his sneakers, scraped his feet on the pavement, saying nothing.

251

We sat like that for a while. The breeze started nipping, and I shivered.

He put his arm around me. "We better get going," he said, smoothing the hairs on my arm back down.

We walked down the curved path, spotted only sporadically with light. A lot of the lamps weren't working.

"So what are you gonna do with yourself when I leave?" I asked.

He pressed his fingers into my arm. "Get some sleep."

It was the day before I had to go back to my mother's. I asked Axel why he never sailed his boat. He said it'd never occurred to him, but why not set sail now?

So we did.

An hour and a half later, we sat on the red vinyl cushions on the deck, surrounded by ocean. It was funny; we hadn't used them the whole summer, and now here we were.

The boat swayed more out there, out on the open water. It was kind of like moving slowly in a big rocking chair. I leaned back and looked up at the sun. It didn't seem so harsh or so stinging. For once, it actually appeared to be beaming.

"You decide what to do about school yet?" I asked. "Maybe you can go in January, if you pick one."

He didn't say anything, just stared out at the water.

"Axel?"

He looked startled.

"What's the matter?" I asked.

"I was just thinking about Shakespeare's references to life being a play: 'All the world's a stage, And all the men and women merely players,' 'Life's but a walking shadow, a poor player, That struts and frets his hour upon the stage, and then is heard no more.'"

He hadn't been like this in so long, until the other night at the play. I'd thought he was breaking away from the sorrow, but here it was again.

"Axel, those are just words." I tried to make light of it. "Shakespeare's whole world was the theater. Of course he compared life to the stage. It's like a butcher comparing life to a rump roast."

"Oh, yeah. That's it exactly."

"Anyone can make analogies. Shakespeare just wrote them really well."

"But Shakespeare was right," he said. "We *are* all just players. We have no control. Someone else wrote the script, and we're all at their mercy. It's like the witches in *Macbeth* predicting his fate, luring him to it. The die is cast."

"I'd say Macbeth's fate had more to do with his pushy wife."

"I'd just like some choice. I'd like to write the script for once."

"Then pick up a pen."

"Do you think we can change our destinies?"

"Yeah, of course," I said. "We all have options. We get to choose between doors one through three. But sometimes . . . I guess we don't think through those choices before we act on them."

"Is it taking action or just acting your role?" He stared at the water again. "Anyway, I never saw any doors, so I never got to try their handles to see if they were locked."

God, I hated him talking like this. It scared me. "Axel . . . you had a horrible childhood. But that doesn't mean there aren't any doors now. What about Juilliard?"

He shrugged, looked at the deck. "You were trapped in a box. And so am I. Except that I *can* see, and all too clearly. It's a room with no way out. And even though I know that on the other side of these walls there are incredible things waiting . . . I'll never have them."

I took his hand. "You can have them, if you break down the walls."

He turned to me, his eyes filled with pain and tears, and shook his head. "I can't."

I learned close, my lips almost brushing his. "You can," I whispered.

I kissed him.

His lips were gentle and sweet, like he was. They felt like shelter.

Our kiss deepened, our tongues comfortable, compatible mates.

A warm tingle spread through me. Not unbridled lust, but a powerful, growing love.

This was it. What I'd been looking for all along. I'd almost rushed right past it, trying to be someone I wasn't ready to be.

He stopped, then ran his fingers down my cheek. "I can't . . . I can't make love with you. I swear to God, Willow, I want to. But I just can't."

"It's okay," I said, kissing his lips lightly. "This is all I need."

We lay on the cushions, kissing, necking, touching, and holding each other in a whole new way for us. This was so different from the gentle hugs and protective caresses that had been a part of our friendship. It was a new level of connection, one we hadn't known before. And the water rocked us, and the breeze fanned us; and for once, the world was on our side.

We kissed for hours, until my stomach growled. We laughed, and we ate, and then we kissed some more.

"This was the best day of my life," Axel said when we were sailing back.

"Mine, too."

That night, falling asleep in Axel's arms on the barge, I knew that I'd finally come home.

Rounded with a Sleep

28

"Where are you going?" Axel had slept past Aunt Agatha's practicing for the first time ever, and I was up before him, for a change. So he wanted to know where I was off to.

"I'm going over to your boat. I want to get something."

"What's that?"

"*Julius Caesar*. I know there's a quote in there that says we control our own destinies. I just can't remember it."

"C'mere," he said, patting the bed. "Where's your aunt?"

"She went to get coffee."

"Quick, then."

When I got close, he grabbed my arm and pulled me down, kissing me deeply. "I'm sorry we didn't do this sooner," he said, running his fingers through my hair.

He kissed me again.

"I'll be back next weekend," I said.

Then Axel said, "Men at sometime are masters of their

fates. The fault, dear Brutus, is not in our stars, but in ourselves."

"That's it!" I said.

"That's not what Shakespeare thinks. It's what Cassius thinks."

"How do you know that?" *God, he was so exasperating!*

"Because Shakespeare writes overwhelmingly about the futility of man fighting fate. 'Our wills and fates do so contrary run, that our devices still are overthrown; our thoughts are ours, their ends none of our own.'

"And 'What fates impose, that men must needs abide; it boots not to resist both wind and tide' and 'It is the stars, The stars above us, govern our conditions,' and—"

"Oh, I give up," I groaned, giving him a whack on the arm. "I can't match you in the Shakespeare department, and I'm not even gonna try. You want to be gloomy, O Prince of Bleakness, then I guess that's your choice."

The door creaked open. Aunt Agatha headed our way with coffee and rolls for herself and Axel, and a melon cup for me. "Ah, good to see you're finally awake," she said to Axel, as she handed us our food.

"Thanks, Agatha. Sorry I slept through our date," he told her. "I guess I was really beat."

"Don't worry. We have many more dates to look forward to."

Aunt Agatha bit a crust off of her roll, swallowed, and said, "Dear hearts, you're not going to believe this, but my tire rolled off my car again yesterday! I was going up the ramp onto the Queensborough Bridge, and—voom!"

"Oy vey," I said. "What happened?"

"Luckily, it was the time a lot of musicians head into the city. A saxophonist I know passed by while the tow truck was hooking up the VW. He stopped and told me to hop in."

"Uh, Agatha," Axel said, "you might want to consider retirement for your car."

"Why? I think that car has several good years left in it."

"At least have the lug nuts checked a little more often. Tires don't usually fall off cars for no reason," he said.

"You may have a point, love."

Hank was waiting in the parking lot to drive me home. Axel brought my suitcase to the limo while I said good-bye to Aunt Agatha on the front deck.

"I don't know what to say," I told her. "Thanks, I guess."

"You don't need to thank me, darling," she said, giving me a gigantic hug. "It's the other way around. You give my life its real meaning, Willow. *You* really are the music."

She gave me a kiss, and I headed down the ladder. When I got to the end of the dock, I turned around. She stood there, watching me. I waved. "See you next weekend," I shouted.

Axel was standing next to the limo. "Ready?"

"I guess."

He held the door for me, then got in too and shut the door. Falstaff was seated across from us. Axel must have gotten him off the boat for me.

"You taking a ride, Axel?" Hank asked.

"No. Just need a minute. Don't take this personally, Hank." Axel pushed the privacy screen button, and it rose up.

Axel took my face in his hands and drew it to his. We kissed.

"Take care of yourself," he said.

"Gee, you sound so serious. I'm gonna see you in a few days."

"Don't let them get to you at school."

I laughed. "There's only three days this week. I think I can handle it."

He kissed me again, holding me so tight it hurt.

Then he let go, opened the door, and got out. He leaned in, just looking at me with those beautiful, enigmatic green eyes.

"What is it?" I asked.

He shook his head slowly. "Nothing. It's—nothing. Good-bye, Willow."

Then he shut the door.

I let the privacy screen down. "You know how to get to Atlantic Beach?" I asked Hank.

"Yup."

The limo started rolling through the gravel. I looked

through the back window at Axel as he got farther and farther away.

We turned through the gate, into the world again.

I put on my headset, looking forward to hearing Jim. I hadn't had much time to listen to my music lately. Not that I would have traded one minute of the time spent with Axel. But it was good to slip back to my old comfort zone.

I pressed Play, and "When the Music's Over" came on. A sad song, but I loved it.

Hank was yelling over the song. I hit stop, annoyed. I hated it when people insisted on talking to me. *Weren't the headphones a clue that I wanted to veg?*

"What?" I asked.

"I said, you're gonna have lots of reading to do at home."

"Meaning what?" I was being a little snippy and just wanted to get back to my music.

"Aw, I forgot. I wasn't supposed to say anything. Don't tell Axel I ruined the surprise, okay?"

"Hank, you're speaking in tongues. What are you talking about?"

Hank sighed. "Axel's sending all his books home with you. He had a truck pick 'em up this morning. It's meeting us at your house."

"What? Why would he do that?"

"Beats me. He said he didn't need 'em any more. I've got all the Shakespeare in my trunk. He didn't trust those guys with 'em."

My pulse picked up the tempo, and I felt heavy in my chest.

Something was wrong, wrong, wrong.

And Axel had been acting so weird. So . . . final.

I thought of the razor blade. I thought of the rough, raised line on Axel's wrist.

The hairs stood up on my arms.

"Hank, turn around. I have to go back. Hurry!"

He laughed, oblivious to my rising panic. "What'd you forget, a book?"

"Yeah, something like that."

I dug my cell phone out of my pocket, flipped it open, found Axel's number, and hit "Send."

I got his voicemail. "Axel, I'm coming back there. Wait for me. . . . Wait for me, Axel. . . . "

I hit "End," tried again. But his voicemail still picked up.

"Shit, shit, shit!"

"Something wrong?" Hank asked.

"I hope not, Hank. Just hurry up and get me back there."

I jumped out while the car was still coming to a stop. "Hey," Hank called from the window. "You gotta be more careful."

"Listen, Hank. Just go home. Come back tomorrow, okay? I'm staying another day." There was no way I could leave Axel right now.

I ran off before Hank could even reply.

Let Axel be okay. Let him have a more deluxe volume of Shakespeare coming for himself, I begged as I sprinted to the dock.

Aunt Agatha was just coming off it. "Willow, what are you doing back?"

"I can't talk now," I puffed out, running past her.

"Do you want Axel's note?" she called after me.

I stopped. "What?"

"He said something came up, and he had to go away suddenly—his father was coming to get him—and would I give it to you."

I snatched the note from her hand, tore it open.

Dear Willow,

> *Forgive me. I lied. I never went to therapy.*

"Oh my God," I said, scanning more:

> *Death isn't dark, it's just nothing. It's being freed from the pain. You inflict pain to end it. You suffer to end the suffering. "To die, to sleep—to sleep, perchance to dream." Willow, I came here to sleep.*

> *I asked my dad to visit. I want him to find me. To deal with the mess for once. . . .*

I crumpled the letter without reading the rest, shoving it into my pocket, and started running again.

"What is it, Willow?" Aunt Agatha called.

I chucked my cell at her. When she caught it, I said, "Call 911. Send them to Axel's boat. Tell them it's an attempted suicide, and tell them to hurry."

"What do you mean?" Aunt Agatha stared at the phone, flabbergasted. "Where did you get this? How do you use it?"

"From Axel." There was no time to answer the first question. "Just flip it open, hit 9-1-1, and 'Send.'"

I ran toward Axel's boat.

�֍

I was too late.

Axel lay on his bedroom floor, engulfed in his own seeped blood. There was so much blood, I couldn't see where it came from. But I knew.

He had to be dead. *You couldn't lose that much blood and live.*

Could you?

I knelt beside him, touched his cheek. He was cold, so cold.

I felt his neck for his pulse.

It was there.

He was alive.

"Oh, Axel . . ." I held back my tears. They were of no use to him.

I grabbed two towels from the bathroom and stretched his arms above his head. Then I knelt between them and pressed a towel on each of his wrists, pushing up his hands at the same time to try and close the grotesque gaps he'd sliced into himself.

I sat in Axel's sea of blood, pressing, pushing, and pleading. "Axel, please, stay with me. Please . . ."

His hair was soaked, matted in red ooze. His arms were unevenly tinged and splattered, like a child had brushed them with a cheap watercolor crimson and would need several more coats to do the job.

His face looked like an angel's. He looked peaceful, blissfully asleep. . . . *Was he dreaming?*

"Please, Axel . . ." My tears came. I couldn't fight them anymore.

I bent by his head. My hair hung low over my face, swinging through blood back and forth like a pendulum. I kissed his forehead. Droplets of blood landed and dripped down the sides of his face.

My legs, arms, and fingers were sticky. My clothes were permeated with red.

My tears dripped into Axel's blood, disappearing into it.

I felt light-headed, like maybe this was all a dream.

Perchance to dream . . .

"Why . . . why did he do this?" Aunt Agatha spoke from the doorway behind me.

"He planned it," I answered. "He . . . he came here to die."

She moved around me, into my view. "He had *every-thing* to live for." Her voice cracked with emotion.

Axel's story spilled from my mouth. I told her in condensed form: his childhood, his self-mutilation, his hopelessness. I ended with how Axel wanted his father to find him.

"And it's my fault he did this. . . . I couldn't help him." His hands were so damn cold, I felt like he was slipping away from me. I pushed them harder toward the wrists, leaned with every bit of strength I had on the towels to try and stop the bleeding.

"He did so much for me, but I couldn't help him," I said.

"He needed more help than you could give him, Willow," Aunt Agatha said quietly.

"He told me he was going to therapy. . . . He lied to me!"

"Don't be angry with him."

"I'm not angry. . . . I'm just . . . oh, God . . . I love him. . . ."

Loud stomping noises came from above. The paramedics had arrived.

"You go with him to the hospital, Willow. I'll meet you there. But first, I'd like a word with the almighty Mr. Ridge."

There Is the World Itself

It had been a whole year, but I couldn't stop thinking about Axel.

Every day, I thought back to the last time I saw him. I watched the paramedics bandage his wrists. And I followed as they rushed him off the boat and down the dock on the stretcher. I held his cold hand on the five-minute ride to the hospital—the one he'd refused to let them take me to.

It wasn't that bad that I could see. Not that I could see much through my tears. I chased the paramedics as they wheeled him down a hall, until some nurse stopped me and said I couldn't go with him any farther.

And then Axel was gone. Just like that. I never got to see him again, never got to give him one last kiss.

At least I knew he was alive. Another nurse came out and told me that much. She told me too that it takes about an hour to bleed out through the veins, and the arteries do it in twenty minutes. Axel had been alone for about half an hour, so I guessed he'd hit a vein.

Knowing he'd survived, I sank into oblivion.

❈

I sat in the emergency waiting room, covered in Axel's blood, and I cried. Blurry people came in and out; I couldn't tell you what anyone looked like. I couldn't describe the room or anything about the hospital at all, other than that it seemed smaller than the one I'd been in.

I slumped in a plastic chair attached to a whole row of chairs. I stared at the TV without knowing what I was seeing—that was blurry, too.

Nothing mattered, anyway.

Nothing mattered but Axel.

Then someone came and sat next to me and took my hand. It was Aunt Agatha. And she spoke to me, but I couldn't take in what she said.

We waited and waited together, and all I wanted was to see Axel. But then a nurse came and told us he'd been moved. His father had called and had him taken away, whisked him off to who knew where. While I was glad he didn't have to stay in this hospital he hadn't wanted me to come to, I knew I wouldn't see him again.

And then I was alone.

All I had were his books and the note he'd left me. I carried it everywhere and read it every day:

Dear Willow,

Forgive me. I lied. I never went to therapy.

Death isn't dark, it's just nothing. It's being freed from the pain. You inflict pain to end it. You suffer to end the suf-

fering. "*To die, to sleep—to sleep, perchance to dream.*"
Willow, I came here to sleep.

*I asked my dad to visit. I want him to find me. To deal
with the mess for once.*

*My one regret is the pain I'm causing you. I'm sorry.
It just hurts too much to be here.*

*Forget me, and move on. You deserve more than a
shadow. You'll be happy one day, I know it.*

*I meant what I said about yesterday being the best day
of my life. Thank you for that. It was the perfect way to say
good-bye.*

I love you,
Axel
PS: I hope you were right about the lobsters.

But then, after a couple of months, I heard from him.

He sent me a postcard with a picture of the Alps, post-
marked in Switzerland. There was no return address.

He wrote:

Willow,

I'm sorry I haven't been in touch.

*I'm feeling really bad, and I don't have it in me to call,
or even to talk.*

I want you to know that I think of you every day.
Love, Axel

It should've made me happy, getting that card. And
maybe it did for, like, five minutes.

But then I got sad again—and very angry.

Angry because I couldn't respond—I couldn't communicate with him at all.

Why didn't he give me his stupid address? It wasn't like I could just hop on a plane and show up there or something.

I guessed he didn't really want me writing to him. He'd completely shut me out, and I didn't understand it. And it hurt so much.

Did he suppose that it would make me feel good—knowing that he was thinking of me? It didn't.

What the hell good were his thoughts doing me? I wanted to hear his voice and be able to touch him. . . .

What if I never touched him again?

I called Mr. Ridge's company and left messages, trying to find out where in Switzerland Axel was. But nobody ever called back.

I got two more cards after that—one about three months later and another three months after that.

Each had that same Alps picture.

Each had no return address.

Each said simply, "Love, Axel."

Part of me wanted to rip them up. A bigger part couldn't.

I decided to listen to my therapist—to try and simply accept the love he'd sent me.

Some days that worked.

Some days it didn't.

School was still the same, but at least Axel had been right about one thing: I didn't gain all the weight back. But I ate, though I made sure to eat, because I knew that he'd want me to.

Even if I was pissed and lonely without Axel, I still owed it to him to take care of myself. He'd helped me so much and in so many ways.

Mom was doing better. At least she was only one person, anyway. She was kind of a flatliner, actually, but whatever. She came home earlier, and we'd go to the diner and talk about not much, but at least it was something. It might have been better if I'd felt like talking. But I didn't.

I didn't hear from my dad. And it was better that way. It was so much better for him to not contact me at all, instead of making plans and then not showing up.

Every Friday after school, Aunt Agatha picked me up at my mom's and brought me to the barge to help and to stay with her for the weekend. Each week, I arrived to find more of the walls covered in mahogany. A mahogany floor was taking shape, and a brick fireplace had been installed. New windows gleamed along the walls, and up front, where the stage was going to be, a humongous picture window had been installed. And the formerly dirty, stained ceiling was now coated in thick white swirls of stucco.

The barge was like Cinderella transformed, but I remained in tatters.

Axel's boat was gone. Back to Manhattan, I guessed. I wondered if his blood came off everything—probably to the naked eye, it did. You might need one of those crime scene investigation tools to detect the bloodstains on the floor. I heard that they never completely come out.

I wondered if Axel's dad let the boat's name stay the same.

I wondered if Axel's dad cared about him now.

I cried at my weekly therapy sessions.

I cried on the barge when I went to sleep, clutching Axel's pillow. It still smelled like him.

I cried in my room when I went to bed, hugging Falstaff. A bright yellow wall faced me where Jim's poster had been. I just couldn't look at it.

Summer came, and once again, I lived on the barge.

In August, the work was finished. It had been just over a year, and the barge was ready to move to its new home.

We were to be towed to Brooklyn by tugboat—a red one like you see on the river. *The Music Barge* was embarking on a six-hour journey from Queens through Long

271

Island Sound and around the Statue of Liberty to the East River.

"Excited?" Aunt Agatha asked, giving me a squeeze.

"Yeah." I traced my foot on a sandy-colored mahogany strip. The center of the room seemed so vacant without the piles of plywood, bundles of mahogany, supplies, and power tools, not to mention Aunt Agatha's cot and my couch, both of which had been moved to her new house in Brooklyn.

Now there were wooden folding chairs stacked in the corner, mahogany benches lining the walls, and red velvet cushions piled on the benches, waiting to be placed on the chairs when they were set up for ticket holders.

"We've already got a full house for the opening concert, plus every performance for the first three weeks! That advance write-up in *The New York Times* sure helped."

"Great," I said, moving my foot to the next strip of wood, this one in more of a maple syrup color.

"Wow, kiddo. I hope the audience is more enthusiastic than that."

"I'm sorry—" I couldn't break out of my permanent mope, even though I really was glad her dream was coming true.

She gave me a rap on the back. "I understand, love."

"When are we leaving?"

"I have a few things to take care of first. And we're moving the barge with a guest. My assistant musical director."

Now *this* was big news. "When did you get an assistant?"

"Just yesterday. He contacted me unexpectedly, and his qualifications were absolutely perfect."

"You hired him over the phone?"

She nodded proudly. "I did."

Aunt Agatha used a cell phone these days. She'd become convinced of the importance of communication when she'd called 911 that day a year ago. Now she handled all her business that way. It was a little scary, watching her fall in with the times. What would be next? A refrigerator? A shower?

"You know," I said, "you ought to get to know someone a little before you hire them." *Yeesh, did I really have to tell her this?*

"You don't trust my instincts?" she asked.

Thinking of Craig, I said, "No."

"Well, we'll have more than six hours to see if we like him. If not, we can set him adrift."

I laughed.

The new steel doors on either end of the barge were very easy to open—unlike their predecessors—with their push bars on the inside and shiny new knobs on the outside. The doors hardly made a sound when you opened them, except for a tiny squeak.

And now the front one squeaked.

"Ah, here he is now," Aunt Agatha said.

Super. I wasn't in the mood for making small talk with some strange dude for six hours. *If I'd known about this in advance, I wouldn't have gone along on this voyage.*

I faced the huge rear window, staring out at the water and the boats. I couldn't see it from that angle, but I knew there was a schooner in Axel's spot.

"Willow, say hello to my assistant."

I didn't feel like turning around. People generally sucked. The mahogany floor creaked with footsteps that came closer to me.

"Hello, Willow," a soft, familiar voice said right behind me.

Oh my God. Axel!

He touched my shoulder and ran his fingers down my arm, raising a line of goose bumps.

"I missed you," he said.

I turned around and embraced him, like he might disappear if I didn't hold tight. He wrapped his warm arms around me, and I leaned my head against his chest, listening to his heartbeat, inhaling his scent.

Neither of us said anything. We didn't need to speak.

"I'll leave you two alone," Aunt Agatha said. "I have to tend to a few details before we depart."

The door squeaked again.

We still didn't say a word. I wanted to hold him like that forever.

I closed my eyes and felt the rhythm of the barge rocking, along with the rhythm of his pulse.

"I'm sorry," he finally said. "I shouldn't have lied to you."

"It doesn't matter," I said.

"I wanted to call you, Willow. But I was just so depressed."

"It doesn't matter."

"So, what does matter?"

"That you're back. That you don't ever—ever do anything like that again!" I tilted my head, ran my hands through his hair, and draped them around his neck to pull him down. "It matters that you kiss me right now."

Everything bad melted away in that moment when our lips met again.

After a few more kisses, I had to ask him a question. "Are you okay now?" I asked, holding his hand and looking into his eyes as I rubbed my thumb along the thicker, rougher line across his wrist.

He nodded. "I'm in therapy—for real, this time. I was at a clinic when I wrote you from Switzerland. I just left it three weeks ago. They helped me—a lot. And now I see a psychologist in the city. And my dad . . . he's actually been pretty cool. Your aunt really got to him. I'm not sure what Agatha said to him, but whatever it was, it shook him. She actually got through to him and made him understand things. I'm not saying we're close, exactly, but . . . it's gotten a lot better."

"So . . . I don't have to worry?"

"No. Not anymore."

And that's when the tears started flowing.

"Just when I thought you'd made such progress," he said, wiping away my drops.

"You started it," I said, wiping at his.

We laughed and kissed again.

"Ahem." Aunt Agatha cleared her throat behind us.

We broke apart. "I'm sorry, Agatha—" Axel said. "We've never done anything more than kiss, honest!"

"Relax, my dear boy," Aunt Agatha said with a laugh. "I'm just relieved you two finally realized you're in love."

"Aunt Agatha!" I was shocked by her approval.

"Darling, did it ever occur to you that I, too, was once young?" She waltzed over and socked Axel playfully on the arm. "Welcome home, dear heart."

"Yeah," I said, giving him another quick kiss. "Welcome home."

Axel and I stood on the back deck as the barge headed out slowly from the dock. We floated away, arms around each other, bouncing lightly on the waves, watching the boatyard retreat until we couldn't see it at all.

"What are you thinking about?" Axel asked, leaning his head against mine.

"There was this Shakespeare quote that kept running through my head while you were gone," I said. "Where thou art . . ."

"There is the world itself," Axel finished. He hugged me hard. "Willow, I'm so sorry. . . ."

"I told you never to be sorry," I reminded him.

We passed under a railroad bridge. The men in the control booth above it waved at us. We waved back.

"Thanks for saving me," Axel said.

"You're welcome," I answered.

We bopped on a big wave, courtesy of a passing schooner. I looked into Axel's eyes. There was no more pain or emptiness. And the intensity I saw there and could hear in his voice was all good now. He was happy—to be home, to be with me.

"I won't leave you again," he said. "That's a promise."

"I know."

And I did.

What's Past Is Prologue

Axel and I clamber up the steel steps to the roof of the barge. The October evening air is tinged with a brisk breeze. We lean against the railing, inhaling the scents and the sights. The water flows silently below us, and across the river, the Manhattan skyline twinkles bewitchingly.

Twilight is here. Tiny headlights cross the Brooklyn Bridge. Cars cross the span, sounding like bees swarming.

Axel's tired. It's tough working for Aunt Agatha and studying at Juilliard, but he's incredibly satisfied in doing both. We'll leave soon, so he can get some rest. We just like a few minutes alone on the roof after every concert.

We stand there, holding hands.

A sight-seeing boat passes by, sending surges of waves our way.

Seagulls circle above the seaport pier across the river, ever waiting for scraps, ever hopeful.

We hold hands, rock on the waves, watch the world before us.

It's not dark after all.

Author's Note

Saved by the Music is a work of fiction. However, it's based on my relationship with my aunt, Olga Bloom, and my experiences working with her to convert a dilapidated coffee barge into the world's first floating concert hall. I was only nine years old, but I did a lot of the work described in this book, including painting the roof! My aunt still has my paint-stained Keds.

Aunt Olga taught me by example that anything is possible if you truly believe and are willing to work relentlessly to make it happen. I can't thank her enough.

For over thirty years, **Bargemusic** has provided audiences with chamber music at least twice a week, all year round. And just as described in *Saved by the Music*, **Bargemusic** is located at Fulton Ferry Landing on the East River in Brooklyn, not far from the Brooklyn Bridge. Visit www.bargemusic.org to learn more about it.

ACKNOWLEDGMENTS

Thanks to Evelyn M. Fazio for kind editing and for
believing in my writing;
Bunny Gabel and Hettie Jones for lighting the path as I
wrote this first novel;
my many friends—writing and otherwise—
for their endless support and always available shoulders;
my mom for exposing me to the arts and supporting my
earliest writing endeavors;
and, of course, my beloved Casey and Michael—
who have the fortune and misfortune to be
the children of a writer.